The Radio Boys at the Sending Station; Or, Making Good in the Wireless Room

by Allen Chapman

Table of Contents

CHAPTER I

THE COLLISION

"Isn't it a grand and glorious feeling?" exclaimed Bob Layton, a tall stalwart lad of fifteen, as he stretched himself out luxuriously on the warm sands of the beach at Ocean Point and pulled his cap a little further over his eyes to keep out the rays of the sun.

"I'll tell the world it is," agreed Joe Atwood, his special chum, as he burrowed lazily into the hollow he had scooped out for himself. "You don't have to put up any argument to prove it, Bob. I admit it from the start."

"Same here," chimed in Herb Fennington, sprawled out in a fashion which if certainly inelegant was quite as certainly comfortable. "Take it from me, it's great. I could die loafing like this."

"Seems to be unanimous," remarked Bob, "although I haven't heard Jimmy's musical voice mixing into the conversation and he's usually right there with the talk. I wonder——"

Just then he was interrupted by a vigorous snore proceeding from a fourth member of the group, a fat round-faced boy slightly younger than the others, who was lying on his back a few feet away.

The boys broke into a laugh.

"There's the answer," chuckled Herb. "Trust Jimmy to go to sleep on the slightest provocation. There's only one thing he can do better, and that is eating."

"He sure is no slouch at either," laughed Joe. "The seven sleepers of Ephesus had nothing on Jimmy. And if he went into a doughnut-eating contest, I'd back him to my last dime."

"It's no wonder that's he's tired," said Bob, coming to the defense of the unconscious Jimmy. "If either of you fellows had had the tussle he had with the waves that night when he was hanging on to the broken bridge expecting every minute to be his last, you wouldn't be feeling any too lively, you can bet your boots."

"Right you are," admitted Herb. "That was a tough fight. It makes the cold chills run up and down my back now when I think of it. I don't think there'll be many times in Jimmy's life when he'll come so near death and yet side-step it."

"You were pretty close to it yourself, Bob," put in Joe. "Your chances of getting by didn't seem to be worth a plugged nickel. Of course you're stronger than Jimmy and could have kept up longer if you'd been swept away, but I don't believe there's any one living that could have bucked that torrent."

"I'll admit that I felt mighty good when I got my feet on solid ground again," said Bob. "There's no denying that that was a pretty strenuous night, what with fighting the waves and Dan Cassey too. But we beat them both and came through all right."

"Talking of Cassey," said Joe, "I saw the rascal this morning when I went into the town to attend to a little business for my father. I wasn't far from the jail and I dropped in to see just what arrangements had been made for his trial. The warden was glad to see me—you know he's been pretty strong for us since we saved the police the work of getting their claws on Cassey—and as he was just about to make the rounds he asked me to go along. So I had a chance to see Cassey behind the bars."

"I suppose he was glad to see you?" remarked Bob, with a grin.

"Tickled to death," laughed Joe. "I'm just as popular with him as poison ivy. He got just purple with rage and shook the bars of his cell as though he were trying to break them to get at me. He tried to tell me what he thought of me, but he stuttered so much that he couldn't get it out. I suppose he's stuttering yet."

"It's not surprising that he's sore at us," said Bob. "That's twice we've put a spoke in his wheel; once when he tried to swindle Miss Berwick in the matter of that mortgage and again when he blackjacked Harvey and looted his safe. We sure have been a jinx for him."

"And he isn't the only one who has it in for us," said Joe, as he caught sight of three boys of about their own age who were passing by, and who in passing cast looks of dislike on the little group on the sands. "There's a sweet bunch—I don't think."

The others followed the direction of Joe's glance and had no trouble in agreeing with him.

"That Buck Looker is sure bad medicine," remarked Bob. "And Lutz and Mooney who hang out with him are just about as bad. They're all tarred with the same brush."

"They're a blot on the landscape—or perhaps I should say seascape," put in Herb.

"Where every prospect pleases,

And only man is vile,"

chanted Joe. "Do you notice how everybody steers clear of them? Outside of each other, not one of them has a friend in the whole colony."

"It's a wonder we haven't had a run in with them before this," ruminated Herb.

"I guess Buck doesn't want any of our game," Joe rejoined. "He's already had one licking from Bob, and it was only the butting in of Mr. Preston that saved him from getting another one from me. But I have a hunch that he'll get it yet. My knuckles are itching, and that's a bad sign—for Buck."

"You'll get the chance all right," predicted Herb. "Ten to one they're framing up some low-down game to play on us whenever they find an opening. Maybe they'll try to put our radio set out of commission, just as they stole Jimmy's set and tried to wreck Bob's aerial."

"They're welcome to try," said Bob carelessly. "Though they ought to be cured of that idea when they remember how they flivvered the other times. But talking of radio reminds me that we ought to get busy with that lightning arrester we were talking about."

"What has lightning done that it ought to be arrested?" joked Herb.

For answer, Bob scooped up a handful of sand and threw it at the scoffer. Herb ducked adroitly and the sand passed over his head and fell full on Jimmy's mouth, which at the moment happened to be open.

There was a terrific coughing and sputtering, as Jimmy came up to a sitting posture with a quickness that was quite foreign to his nature.

"Who—who the mischief did that?" he demanded, as soon as he could speak, glaring indignantly from one to the other of his comrades, who at first had been alarmed for fear he would choke but now were convulsed with laughter.

"I did," confessed Bob, as he tried to restrain his untimely mirth. "But I didn't mean to, old scout. Herb here had just gotten off one of his horrible jokes, and I was trying to make the punishment fit the crime. I'm awfully sorry."

"You look it," snorted Jimmy, still trying to get the remainder of the sand out of his mouth. "You look as though your heart was broken, sitting there and grinning like a monkey."

"Cross my heart and hope to die, I didn't mean to," declared Bob. "I wouldn't have disturbed your innocent slumbers for anything in the world."

"Never mind, Jimmy," put in Herb. "They say that every one has got to eat a peck of dirt before they die, and you might as well start in early."

"I guess I got my whole peck then," grumbled Jimmy, as he rubbed his mouth vigorously with his handkerchief. "I feel like a chicken with sand in its craw."

"You ought to feel pretty good then," replied Herb, "for they eat it because they like it."

"You're the cause of it all," said Jimmy. "When you try to be funny again, do it when I'm not around. I'll bet the joke was a rotten one, anyway."

"Shall I tell it to you?" asked Herb hopefully.

"Not unless you're prepared to die," replied Jimmy, and Herb forebore to add insult to injury.

"Now as to this lightning arrester," resumed Bob, leaving Jimmy to regain his equanimity. "We've got to put it up, for the regulations require it and we ought to have done it before."

Jimmy pricked up his ears but said nothing.

"I don't think there's really much need of it," objected Joe. "It's too nice an afternoon to work. We've got a lightning rod on the cottage anyway."

"It isn't so much for the cottage as the set," said Bob. "If the lightning got into the receiving set it would make short work of it. Now here's the kind of lightning switch we'll have to have," and he launched into an earnest discussion of a type that was required by the radio regulations.

Jimmy took no part in the discussions, but they attributed this to a touch of grouchiness and gave him time to get over it. Bob after a while glanced at him, and saw that he wore a broad grin on his face.

"What's the joke, Jimmy?" he asked, a little suspiciously.

For only answer Jimmy broke into a peal of laughter.

"Of all the boobs," he chortled.

They looked at him and then at each other in bewilderment.

"Do you think the sun has affected his brain?" asked Herb, with affected anxiety.

"It might have, if he had any brain to be affected," replied Joe, in the same strain.

"Let us in on it, Jimmy," pleaded Bob. "Don't be selfish and keep it all to yourself."

"Why, you thick heads," replied Jimmy, with more force than politeness, "don't you know that you don't have to have a lightning arrester with a loop aerial?"

There was a moment's silence while they let this sink in, and then a sheepish grin stole into their faces.

"Sure enough," owned up Bob. "I knew that too, but I had forgotten it for the time. I was thinking of the outdoor aerial. Of course on an indoor aerial there's no need of a lightning arrester. Jimmy, I take off my hat to you. As the leader of the lynching party said to the widow, after they had lynched the wrong man, the joke's on us."

"I guess that evens things up," crowed Jimmy gleefully, his usual good-humor completely restored. "To think of all that waste of good chin music over nothing," he added mockingly.

"Don't rub it in," admonished Joe. "We'll admit that we're boobs and let it go at that. Serves us right for thinking of working on a day like this, anyway. Those people out there have the right idea," he continued, pointing to a party in a rowboat some distance out from the shore.

"Wish we were out there with them," remarked Herb enviously, as his eyes followed the boat, which had in it three persons, two boys and a girl.

"A sailboat would be good enough for me," put in Jimmy. "Rowing is too much like work."

"Or better yet a motor boat like that one coming over from the right," said Herb. "In that thing the engine does all the work."

"Those fellows in the rowboat seem to be laboring pretty hard at the oars," remarked Bob. "They don't seem to be any too expert, and the waves are pretty rough since that wind sprang up."

"The reason they're pulling so hard is to get out of the way of that motor boat," declared Joe. "It looks almost as though they were going to run them down."

"There wouldn't be any excuse for that with the whole broad ocean to maneuver in," commented Bob. "But, Great Scott!" he cried, jumping to his feet. "That's just exactly what it's doing. Look! It's right on top of them!"

The four boys watched with breathless interest the unfolding before their eyes of what promised to be a tragedy.

The young men in the smaller boat were pulling like mad to get out of the way of the motor boat bearing down upon them with undiminished speed. The girl in the stern of the boat was wringing her hands and screaming.

Whether the two men in the motor boat failed to see the rowboat in their path, or whether they were simply reckless and heartless, it was impossible to tell. In any event, there was no shifting of the helm, no slackening of speed. Swift and relentless as doom the motor craft drove into the rowboat and crushed it like an eggshell.

CHAPTER II

TO THE RESCUE

There was a gasp of horror from the boys as they saw the three forms struggling in the water amid the débris of the shattered rowboat.

"They'll be drowned!" shouted Bob, in an agony of apprehension.

"If they can only keep afloat until the motor boat picks them up," ejaculated Joe.

But to the consternation of the boys they saw that the motor boat occupants had no intention of going to the rescue. It was not that the men on the boat were not aware of the damage they had done. The boys could see the figures of two men looking backward from the stern towards the people struggling in the waves. But there was no halting of the speed of the craft and it kept on like an arrow, as though it were a criminal bent only on getting away from the scene of his crime.

A cry broke from the boys when this conviction was forced upon them. They clenched their fists and shook them toward the retreating craft, while fierce exclamations broke from their lips.

But there was no time for indulging in vain objurgations. Bob as usual took the lead.

"Come along, fellows!" he shouted, as he set off like a deer towards a rowboat that was pulled up on the beach. "We've got to save those people, and every second counts. Hustle's the word!"

His companions were close on his heels, and without loss of time they had reached the boat. In it were two pairs of oars. They pushed the boat down the shelving beach into the surf and jumped aboard.

"Each one take an oar," commanded Bob. "Now pull, fellows, with all your strength. Don't mind about the steering. I'll tend to that. Pull! Pull!"

They did not need any urging, and the boat, yielding to the impetus of four pairs of arms, made rapid headway and had soon got beyond the breakers. But the tide was setting toward the shore and the waves were running high, while the wind was strong and against them. Filled with anxiety as they were, it seemed to them that the boat was only creeping, though they were putting their arms and their backs into the work and pulling with every ounce of strength that they possessed.

Bob used his oar both for pulling and steering, and ever and again cast a glance behind him to make sure of his course. He could see that the two men had caught hold of a fragment of the boat and were trying to keep afloat. The girl seemed to have fainted and was supported by the arm of one of the men. As the waves rolled toward them, they tried to rise with them, but often they were entirely submerged, and there was danger that at any moment their hold might be torn from the slight fragment that alone kept them afloat.

The need for haste was urgent, and Bob urged his comrades on with frantic adjurations.

"Pull harder," he cried, himself setting the example. "Harder yet. Put all you've got into each stroke. Harder! Harder!"

It seemed as though their hearts were being pulled out of their bodies, but they summoned up all their strength for a final spurt that carried them into the floating débris of the boat.

"Easy now," cried Bob, as he shipped his oar. "You, Herb and Jimmy, just row enough to keep her head on. Joe, give me a hand."

He reached out and caught the arm of the lad who was supporting the girl. While Bob held him fast, Joe reached over, took his helpless burden from his arms, and lifted her into the boat. That done, they reached over and helped the nearly exhausted youths into the boat with what aid they themselves were able to render. They were too used up to talk, but their eyes showed their gratitude.

"Well, that's that!" exclaimed Bob, heaving a sigh of heartfelt relief, as he again took up his oar. "Now, fellows, it's us for the shore as soon as we can get there. These people are all in and need first aid, especially the girl. Let's go."

9

With tired arms and bodies but vastly lighter hearts, they bent to the oars.

And while they are speeding over the waves with their burden, it may be well, for the benefit of those who have not read the previous volumes of this series, to tell who the radio boys were and what had been their adventures up to the time this story opens.

Bob Layton was the son of a prosperous chemist living in the town of Clintonia, a thriving community of about ten thousand population, situated on the Shagary River in an Eastern state, about seventy-five miles from New York. Bob had been born and brought up there, and was a general favorite with the people of the town, especially the boys of his own age, because of his sunny nature and frank, straightforward character. He was a natural leader in all wholesome sports and a crack player on the school baseball and football teams.

His special chum was Joe Atwood, a boy of about his own age and the son of a leading doctor of the town. While both were tall, Joe was of a fair complexion while Bob was dark, and the dissimilarity extended to other things than mere appearance. Joe was impulsive and quick-tempered, and apt to act on the spur of the moment, while Bob, although never shirking trouble or a fight if it came his way, was more self-controlled. But their points of likeness were more numerous than their points of difference, and they were the warmest of friends. Where one was to be found the other was usually not far off.

Closely associated with them were Herb Fennington and Jimmy Plummer, slightly younger but nearly enough of an age to be good comrades. Jimmy was round and fat and fond of good living, a trait which had earned him the nickname of "Doughnuts." Herb was rather easy-going and fond of telling jokes, of which he always had a stock in store.

In one way or another the four friends frequently came into conflict with Buck Looker, the bully of the town, and his two boon companions, Carl Lutz and Terry Mooney, who were of the same stripe, though they deferred to Buck as their leader.

Ever since the wonderful new science of radio had come into such worldwide prominence, Bob and his friends had been intensely interested in it. That interest had been fostered by the stimulating advice and information given them by Dr. Amory Dale, the pastor of the old First Church of Clintonia. How they had made their own receiving sets in competition for the prize offered by the member of Congress for their district; the difficulties they surmounted and the triumphs they achieved; how Buck and his gang sought to wreck and steal their sets and the thrashing Buck received in consequence; how by the agency of the radio they were able to detect a swindler, one, Dan Cassey, and force him to make restitution to Nellie Berwick, an orphan girl he had tried to cheat; all this and many more exciting adventures are told in the first book of this series, entitled: "The Radio Boys' First Wireless; Or, Winning the Ferberton Prize."

The winning of the prizes, the first by Bob and the second by Joe, with honorable mention for Jimmy, was a spur to fresh efforts in mastering the wonders of radio. This they carried out at Ocean Point, a seashore resort, at which they spent their vacation. How they advanced to the use of the vacuum tube receiving set from their first crystal set; their experiences in the wireless room of a seashore station; their narrow escape from death on the night of a roaring gale; how, under the stress of need, they were able to send a message to the ship on which relatives and friends were voyaging and bring other ships to their aid; how they tracked down and captured the rascal Cassey after he had assaulted and robbed their friend Brandon Harvey, the wireless operator; these things are narrated in the second volume of this series entitled: "The Radio Boys at Ocean Point; Or, The Message That Saved the Ship."

With the radio boys pulling hard at the oars, it was only a matter of a few minutes before they had made their way through the breakers and reached the shore. There they jumped out and shoved the rowboat up on the beach.

The youths whom they had rescued and who seemed only little older than themselves had by this time partially recovered from their exhaustion and were able to get out themselves, although they were very shaky on their legs. The girl had regained consciousness, but was not able to walk, and the boys debated just what they should do.

Quite a crowd that had watched the rescue from the beach were on hand to greet and congratulate them and offers of help were plentiful. But Dr. Atwood, Joe's father, who had taken a day off from his extensive practice to spend it with his family at the Point, solved the problem.

"Bring the girl up to my cottage," he directed. "I'll give her the necessary treatment and then Mrs. Atwood can take charge of her until she's sufficiently recovered to be taken home. I'll give you boys something too that will counteract the effects of the shock and strain you've been under, and you'll be all right in a little while."

The boys picked up the girl and carried her to the Atwood cottage that was only a little distance away. Rose Atwood together with Agnes and Amy Fennington, who had come over and were all interest and attention, recognized her as Mary Rockwell, a girl whom they had met at the dance which the radio boys had given, getting the music over the radio set from a broadcasting station. Together with Mrs. Atwood, they gave her all possible care after the doctor had given her a sedative, and word was sent over to her people assuring them of her safety.

In the meanwhile the rescued lads, after they had been looked over by the doctor and given a slight stimulant, had been borne off bodily by Bob and the other radio boys to the cottage of Bob's parents, where they sat on the veranda while supper was being prepared, for Bob had given them a cordial invitation to take supper and spend the evening with them.

As they were about the size of Bob and Joe, the latter had furnished them with extra suits of their own clothes while their drenched garments were taken in charge by Mrs. Layton to be dried and pressed.

And now for the first time the new acquaintances were able to take a good look at each other. What they saw pleased them mutually.

One of the boys was slender and agile, with frank, honest eyes and a friendly smile that was almost constantly in evidence. His hair was brown and wavy and

11

his complexion naturally fair, though it was at the moment tanned by the sun and sea air. There was not an ounce of superfluous flesh on his body, and he gave the impression of being a trained athlete.

The other had a humorous face that betrayed Irish ancestry, which was emphasized by the merest touch of a brogue when he talked. His hair was red and his face freckled, and there was something about him that was extremely likable and made the boys warm to him at once.

"We haven't had a chance to learn each other's names yet," said Bob, with a smile, as the party settled comfortably into the veranda seats. "And that's not surprising either," he added, "for we've been pretty busy since the first moment we met. This is the first chance we've had to draw our breaths. My name is Bob Layton, and these pals of mine are Joe Atwood, Herb Fennington and Jimmy Plummer, the latter the greatest doughnut eater in captivity."

"And our handles are Larry Bartlett and Tim Barcommon," said the taller of the two newcomers, as they laughingly acknowledged the introductions. "And before we do anything else we want to tell you fellows how grateful we are for the way you came to our help. It would have been all up for us if you hadn't."

"Yes," chimed in Tim, "we'll never forget it as long as we live. It was a mighty plucky thing for you fellows to pull out in the sea that was running. The sight of you coming was the only thing that helped me to hold on. I was just about all in when you reached us. You certainly sent that old boat spinning along."

"Oh, that was nothing," disclaimed Bob. "We just happened to be on the spot. Any one else would have done the same thing."

"But you notice nobody else did do it," replied Larry. "There were lots of other people on the beach that saw the accident, but you were the only ones that did the hustling. It was a case of quick thinking as well as plucky acting, and we owe our lives to you. I only hope that some time we'll be able to do something that will show you how we appreciate it."

"What gets me," put in Joe, "was the heartless way those fellows in the motor boat acted. They were simply brutes. They ought to have their necks wrung."

"Yes," said Herb. "There was no excuse for their running you down in the first place. But after they'd done it, the least they could have done was to turn their boat around and pick you up. We took it for granted that that was what they would do, and we couldn't believe our eyes when we saw them keep on. Those fellows are nothing less than murderers."

"I guess you're about right," replied Larry. "We counted, too, on their picking us up, and our only thought was to hold on to any floating thing we could grab until they could get to us. And when we saw that they weren't going to, we just about gave up hope. Both Tim and I are pretty good swimmers, and if we'd been alone might have reached the shore. But there was the girl, and with the water as rough as it was we had a pretty slim chance of bringing her in, so it was a case of living or dying together. And it would have been dying sure enough, if you hadn't happened to be on the beach this afternoon.

"It would have been especially hard," he continued, "if the girl had been drowned when she was out on our invitation and under our protection. As for ourselves, it would not have mattered so much. She is an awfully nice girl, and her family and mine have been acquainted for years. My mother and hers used to go to school together. I hadn't any idea she was down here when I decided to spend a couple of weeks at Ocean Point, but you can imagine how surprised and delighted I was to find that she and her folks were stopping at the same hotel I had picked out. She was a little afraid of the water, but yielded when we urged her to come out for a row, and we were all having a dandy time until that motor boat come along and spoiled everything."

"And think of what the world would have lost if we'd been among the missing," said Tim, with a grin. "No more exhibitions of the Canary Bird Snake, otherwise known as Larry Bartlett."

"Or of the famous buck wing and clog dancer, otherwise known as Tim Barcommon," laughed Larry.

The radio boys looked at each other in some perplexity.

"I don't quite get you," said Bob.

CHAPTER III

AT THE WIRELESS STATION

"Why, it's this way," explained Larry. "We are vaudeville performers. Tim's specialty is dancing, and I can tell you, because he's too modest to say it himself, that he's a peach. Whenever he appears, he just knocks them off their seats. He's a riot."

"Cut it out," protested Tim. "Leave that to the press agent."

"It's straight goods, just the same," declared Larry. "As for little me, I've got a knack of twisting myself into knots, and then, too, I do a little whistling. And because of that they call me on the posters and in the theater programs the Canary Bird Snake. Kind of mixed up, isn't it?"

The radio boys were tremendously interested. The stage had for them the touch of mystery and glamour that appeals to youth, and it was an unusual treat for them to be talking on familiar terms with characters such as they had only seen hitherto in the glare of the footlights.

"It must be great," said Bob, "to go all over the country as you do and see all there is to be seen."

"Oh, like everything else, theatrical life has its ups and downs," replied Larry. "It's all right when they hand you applause, but not such fun when they throw eggs, especially if the eggs are old. We've never had that experience yet though, and here's hoping that we never shall. There's lots of hard work connected with it, and Tim and I have to work a good many hours each day to keep ourselves in trim. Then, too, when you're playing one night stands and have to get up before daylight to catch a train, which in rube towns often turns out to be just a caboose attached to a freight, it isn't any fun. And it's less fun when you happen to get snowed in for a day or two, as has happened to us several times. But you get paid for all that when your turn goes big and the audience is friendly and gives you a good hand. Oh, it isn't all peaches and cream, but take it altogether we have a pretty good time."

"That is, when we're working," put in Tim. "It isn't much fun though when the ghost doesn't walk every Saturday night."

The boys looked a little puzzled and Larry undertook to enlighten them.

"Tim means when the pay check doesn't happen to come along," he said. "In other words, when we're out of a job. You see we're both pretty young in the profession and we aren't as well known as we hope to be later on. We have to take what we can get on the small-time circuits, and we know that if we make good there we'll get on the big-time circuit sooner or later. Just now things are slack in the theatrical line as they always are in summer. We've got our lines out for a job in the fall, but nothing definite has come of it yet. So we thought we'd come down to the seashore for a few weeks and get a little of the sea air into our lungs."

"But we didn't figure on getting as much sea water into our stomachs as we did this afternoon," laughed Tim. "I can taste it yet. I don't think I'll want any salt on my victuals for a month to come."

Just then Mrs. Layton appeared and announced that supper was ready, and they all obeyed the call with alacrity, Bob's chums being included in the invitation.

The meal was excellent, as Mrs. Layton's always were, and there was a great deal of jollity as it progressed. Larry was very droll and kept the boys in roars of laughter as he told of some of the funny incidents in his experience, and Tim was not far behind him.

After the meal was over, nothing would do but that Larry and Tim should go through some of their performances for the entertainment of the company. This they did, and though they were handicapped by the absence of the usual stage properties, Larry not having his stage suit with him and Tim being without his clog dancing pumps, the spectators were delighted. Larry tied himself into a mystifying tangle of knots, and his whistling was so sweet and melodious that it roused his audience to the heights of enthusiasm. And Tim's graceful dancing was a revelation of the possibilities of the Terpsichorean art.

Then the radio boys took their turn and gave their visitors a radio concert that was wonderful in its variety and beauty. The night happened to be unusually free of the annoying static that is the bugbear of the wireless, and every note of the music was as clear and sweet as though the performers were only a few yards away. Tim and Larry listened as though they were entranced, and when the concert was finished they were as enthusiastic "fans" as the radio boys themselves.

"It's simply wonderful!" exclaimed Larry. "It's the first time I've ever had the chance to 'listen in,' but you can bet it won't be the last."

"I'll tell you what," proposed Bob. "We're going over to the wireless sending station to-morrow morning to see the operator there, Mr. Harvey. He's the finest kind of a fellow, and he'll be glad to see you. Suppose you and Tim come along with us."

"Surest thing you know!" ejaculated Larry, and Tim acquiesced with equal enthusiasm.

They parted for the night with a feeling on both sides of warm liking and esteem and a looking forward to a most enjoyable time on the following day.

The next morning the radio boys set out shortly after breakfast, met Larry and Tim at a point previously agreed upon, and together took their way toward the wireless station.

Mr. Harvey was alone when they entered, and jumped to his feet with hands extended in greeting and a face beaming with welcome.

"What good wind blew you over here?" he exclaimed, as he shook their hands heartily.

"We came because we wanted to see you, and also because we wanted to show our friends here something of the way the wireless works," said Bob.

He introduced Larry and Tim and Mr. Harvey welcomed them so warmly that they felt at once at home.

"So these are the young men you boys pulled out of the water yesterday," he said. "It's mighty lucky for them that you happened to be around."

"I'll say it was," agreed Larry, and Tim nodded vigorously.

"How did you happen to hear of it?" asked Bob.

"Hear of it?" Brandon Harvey repeated. "All the beach is ringing with it. All the hotels are buzzing with it. If you'll look at the morning papers from the city, you'll find they all have a full account of it with comments on the pluck and presence of mind of the fellows who did it. You can't get away with that stuff without having it known, no matter how modest you are."

"Making lots of fuss about a trifle," muttered Bob.

"Trifle," laughed Harvey. "Just the same kind of a trifle as that you pulled off the night you saved the ship and captured the man who had knocked me out. Have they told you about that?" he asked, turning to Larry and Tim.

"Not a word," replied Larry.

"Never breathed it," declared Tim.

"Just like them," asserted Brandon Harvey, and then went on to tell them of that dreadful night when the storm was raging; how they had found him knocked senseless on the floor and the safe looted; how they had sent the signals that had saved the ship from destruction; how they had pursued the robber and captured him after a hand to hand tussle and recovered the loot.

"Well, now about the wireless," interposed Bob, anxious to change the subject. "These friends of ours are a new addition to the army of fans and we want to put them next to some of the wonders of radio."

"It's a great army all right," laughed Harvey, "and we're always glad to welcome new recruits. They're coming into the ranks by thousands every day. Nobody can keep count of them, but they must run into the millions.

"And they're great in quality as well as quantity," he continued, warming to his favorite subject. "The President of the United States has a radio receiving set on his desk. There's one in the office of every one of the ten Cabinet members. The Secretary of the Navy is sending out wireless messages every day to vessels scattered in all parts of the globe. The head of the army is keeping in touch by radio with every fort and garrison and corps area in the United States. On last Arbor Day the Secretary of Agriculture talked over the radio to more people than ever heard an address in the history of the world. But there," he said, breaking off with a laugh, "if I once get going on this line I'll never know when to stop. So I'll say it all in one sentence—the radio is the most wonderful invention ever conceived by the mind of man."

"You don't need to prove it to us," laughed Bob. "It's simply a miracle, and we become more convinced of that every day. I'm mighty glad I was born in this age of the world."

The boys crowded around Mr. Harvey as he explained to Larry and Tim in as simple a way as possible the radio apparatus of the station.

"When I press this key," he said, "an electrical spark is sent up into the antenna, the big wire that you see suspended from the mast over the station, and is flung out into space."

"Travels pretty fast, doesn't it?" asked Larry, to whom all this was new.

"Rather," laughed Mr. Harvey. "It can go seven and a half times around the world while you are striking a match."

"What!" exclaimed Larry incredulously. "Why, the circle of the earth is about twenty-five thousand miles."

"Exactly," smiled Harvey. "And that spark travels at the rate of one hundred and eighty-six thousand miles a second."

"You're sure you don't mean feet instead of miles?" suggested Tim dubiously.

"It's miles all right," laughed Harvey. "Electricity travels at the same rate as the light that comes to us from the sun and stars."

"What becomes of this electrical impulse after it gets started on that quick trip?" asked Larry. "How does the fellow on the other end get what you're trying to tell him."

"That fellow or that station has another antenna waiting to receive my message," replied Harvey. "The signal keeps on going through the ether until it strikes that other antenna. Then it climbs along it until it reaches the receiving set and registers the same kind of dot or dash as the one I made at this end. It's like the pitcher and catcher of a baseball battery. One pitches the ball and the other receives the same ball. At one instant it's in the pitcher's hand and the next it has traveled the space between the two and is resting in the catcher's hand. Sounds simple, doesn't it?"

16

"Sounds simple when you put it that way," laughed Larry. "But I have a hunch that it isn't as simple as it sounds."

"Well, to tell the truth, it isn't quite as simple as that," confessed Harvey. "There's a whole lot to learn about receiving and transmitting and detectors and generators and condensers and vacuum tubes and all that. But my point is that there's nothing of the really essential things that are concerned in getting entertainment and instruction from radio that can't be learned with a little application by any one of ordinary intelligence."

"I wonder if I'm in that class," said Larry quizzically, and there was a general laugh.

Another half hour was spent with great profit and interest in the sending station and then the boys arose to go.

"How are you getting along with that regenerative set?" asked Mr. Harvey of Bob.

"Pretty well, thank you," answered Bob. "It's the proper adjusting of the tickler that's giving me the most trouble."

"Be careful not to increase it too far," warned Harvey. "If you do, the vacuum tube oscillates and becomes a small generator of high frequency current and in that way will interfere with other near-by stations. Then, too, the speeches and music will be mushy instead of being clear. Drop in again when you have time and we'll talk the matter over a little further."

The visitors bade their host farewell and trooped out into the bright sunshine. Larry and Tim were enthusiastic over the new world into which they had been introduced.

"The most wonderful thing in the world," was their verdict.

They spent the rest of the morning on the beach, and before they parted, Larry had secured a promise from the radio boys to come over to a dance that was to be held the next night at the hotel where he and Tim were stopping.

"Jolliest kind of fellows, aren't they?" said Joe.

"They sure are," agreed Herb. "I should think that free and easy life of theirs would be just one round of enjoyment."

"I wouldn't exactly say that," remarked Bob. "Two or three times I have noticed a look of worry in Larry's eyes as though something were weighing on his mind."

This arrow, shot at a venture, was indeed correct, for Larry was far from being as care free as the boys imagined. The fact that he was out of work at present worried him, naturally. But this would have but little weight with him had it not been for his sick mother at home. That mother had worked for years in his behalf, following the death of his father, whose affairs were so involved at his death that there was little money left to support his wife and child. The mother had kept up a brave heart, however, and done the best she could for herself and her idolized son. The strain of being both bread-winner and mother had told, however, and now she was in ill health. Larry, since he had entered upon a profession, had sent to her all that he possibly could in order to maintain her in comfort, but just now the source of supply had stopped and there was no knowing at what time it would be resumed. He knew that his mother had very little money on hand at the time, and her condition of health made Larry her only resource.

The radio boys kept their engagement, and the dance was a jolly affair at which they enjoyed themselves thoroughly. The only drawback to a perfect evening was the fact that Buck Looker and Carl Lutz were there also, but this did not bother them much in the early part of the evening.

The last dance had just been concluded and the ardent dancers were clamoring for one more encore, when a disturbance rose at one end of the room that attracted general attention. The radio boys hurried to the spot in question to find Buck and Lutz talking excitedly while Larry and Tim were standing near them with flushed and indignant faces. The manager of the hotel and a house detective were also in the group.

"I tell you that those are the fellows who did it," Buck was vociferating, while he pointed to Larry and Tim. "They were the ones closest to me when I missed my watch and stickpin, and I had just looked at my watch the minute before. If you search them you'll find the goods on them. My friend here lost his at the same time."

"It's false!" cried Larry.

"If there weren't ladies here, I'd cram the story down your throat!" exclaimed Tim, his eyes blazing.

"That's a serious charge you're making, young man," said the manager to Buck.

"They've got them," said Buck sullenly. "Search them and you'll find I'm right."

"See here," cried Larry. "If this fellow were the only one concerned I wouldn't condescend to satisfy him. But I have some friends here," indicating the radio boys, "and for their sakes I'm going to establish my innocence beyond any doubt. Come right in to one of the private rooms here and search me thoroughly. As for this fellow," glaring at Buck, "I'll settle with him at another time."

The party adjourned to a room, and a thorough search resulted in showing that none of the missing articles was on Larry or Tim.

"Now I'll settle with you," cried Larry, making a rush at Buck. But he was restrained by the house detective who held him while Buck and his crony slunk away.

The radio boys gathered around their new friends and condoled with them over the unfounded accusation.

"He'll pay me for that yet," declared Larry, who had been wrought up to a high pitch of excitement.

"Here's hoping you'll get a hack at him," said Joe. "Did you notice that there wasn't a word of apology for having made a false charge against you?"

"Did you ever know him to do a decent thing?" asked Bob scornfully. "That's Buck Looker to a dot."

The next morning Bob was over at Joe's bungalow when Mr. and Mrs. Rockwell called with Mary to thank the Atwoods for the care they had given Mary when she was brought from the water, and also to express their gratitude to the boys, whose quickness and resource had saved her life.

Mary, a pretty girl, had entirely recovered, and was profuse in her thanks to Bob and Joe, which were echoed by her parents, who laid so much stress upon their bravery that the boys blushed to the ears.

"You are making altogether too much of it," Bob protested, and Joe agreed.

"It is impossible to do that," said Mr. Rockwell, and Mrs. Rockwell nodded her head vigorously.

"The only thing I am sorry about," said Bob, "is that we have not been able to catch the fellows in the motor boat who ran the rowboat down. They ought to be sent to jail on the double quick."

"It turns out," said Mr. Rockwell, "that they were not only heartless brutes, but thieves as well. We found out yesterday that the boat had been stolen from Mr. Wentworth, who is one of the guests at the hotel where we are stopping. They left an old rowboat in its place. Mr. Wentworth has put the police on the track of the thieves, but as yet nothing has been heard of them. I am afraid they have made good their escape."

"I only hope," declared Bob, "that I may live long enough to get my hands on the throat of one or both of them."

"I'd like that privilege," returned Mr. Rockwell warmly, "but I am afraid the chances are slim. They may be hundreds of miles away by this time."

"Well," said Joe, "the arm of the law is long and it may reach them yet."

"Here's hoping," said Bob.

CHAPTER IV

RADIO PLANS

Shortly after the unfortunate affair at the dance Larry and Tim came to the Layton bungalow, overjoyed at a letter they had just received.

"Bob, our streak of bad luck must be broken at last," exulted Larry. "It was beginning to look like the bread line for ours, but now maybe we'll be able to eat heartily again."

"You don't look very hungry just at present," grinned Bob. "But what does it say in that letter that you're waving around, anyway?"

"We've got an engagement, at last," put in Tim. "And, oh, boy! make out it doesn't seem like money from home!"

"Well, that's certainly fine," said Bob, heartily.

"It's with Chasson's vaudeville show," explained Larry. "It's a traveling show, and we probably won't show more than one or two nights in a town. Of course, it isn't as swell an outfit as we would like to connect up with, but it will keep the wolf from the door for a little while."

"It will tide us over until we can hook up with something classier, anyway," said Tim. "The chances are we'll play in all the towns around this part of the country, and if we land in the one you fellows live in, we'll expect you to applaud our act harder than any of the others, no matter how bad we are." And he grinned.

"If you come to Clintonia, you can bet we'll give you the glad hand, all right," promised Bob. "I suppose we all get free passes, don't we?" with a twinkle in his eye.

"You'd get all you want if Tim and I had the say-so," said Larry, "but the manager probably won't be able to see it that way."

"Some day we'll have a show of our own, maybe," said Tim. "Then we'll give you all passes, you can bet your boots on that."

"Don't try to hold your breath until then, though," said Larry. "The way things are breaking for us lately, we'll be more likely to be inviting our friends to come and visit us in the poorhouse."

"Over the hills to the poorhouse,

It's not so far away,

We may get there to-morrow,

If we don't get there to-day,"

chanted Tim, immediately afterward breaking into a lively jig to express his indifference to that mournful possibility.

"Well, if you ever do land in that cheerful place, you'll be very popular," laughed Bob. "But now that you've both got an engagement, you won't have to worry about that for some time to come. I know the other fellows will be glad to hear about it, too. They went down to town this morning, but they ought to be back pretty soon now. Stick around till they come, and we'll tell them the glad news."

"Surest thing you know," acquiesced Larry. "We don't have to report to Chasson until day after to-morrow, anyway. How's the wireless coming along these days?"

"Fine and dandy," responded Bob. "After we get back to Clintonia we intend to build some big sets so that we can receive signals from all over the country."

"But where do you get all the money to buy that stuff?" asked Larry. "Some of it must be pretty expensive, isn't it?"

"Not as expensive as you might think, although some of the apparatus, like audion bulbs, certainly run into money," replied Bob. "But we can easily sell the apparatus that we already have, and make enough on that to buy the new things with. There are plenty of people ready and anxious to buy our sets, because we can sell them for less than the store would charge, and they work as well or better than some store sets."

"Who's talking of selling our sets?" broke in a well-known voice, as Joe, Herb and Jimmy came, pellmell, into the room.

20

"I was," said Bob, in answer to Jimmy's question. "I was thinking of selling your set to the junkman, for what it would bring."

"Huh!" exclaimed Jimmy, indignantly. "I'll bet a junkman wouldn't even buy yours. He'd expect you to pay him to take it away."

"Say, you fellows must have a high opinion of each other's radio outfits," broke in Tim, laughing. "But if you want to give one away, here's Tiny Tim, ready and waiting."

"No chance," said Jimmy, positively. "I worked too many hot nights on mine to give it away now, and I guess Bob thinks he'd like to keep his, too, even though it isn't really much good."

"It was good enough to take the Ferberton prize, anyway, which is more than some people can say of theirs," Bob replied, grinning. "How about it, Doughnuts?"

"That was because the judges didn't know any better," said his rotund friend. "They should have made me the judge, and then there's no doubt but what my set would have won that hundred bucks."

"We can believe that easily enough," laughed Larry. "But you radio bugs forget your hobby for a few minutes and listen to the glad news," and then he told them about the engagement he and Tim had secured.

All the boys congratulated them on their good fortune, and after some further conversation the two actors departed, first promising to drop in for a visit before going away to start their engagement.

"I like those two fellows first rate, and would be mighty glad to see them succeed," said Bob, after they had gone. "It seems to me they ought to make a big hit, too. They're a regular riot all the time they're with us."

"Yes, they're certainly funny," agreed Joe. "What were you telling them about selling our sets, just as we came in?"

"Oh, I was just saying that we could get money to buy new apparatus, audion bulbs, and that sort of expensive stuff, by selling one or two of the sets we've got now, and whacking up the proceeds," said Bob. "My dad spoke of that last evening, and it struck me as a mighty good idea. I know of several people in Clintonia who would like nothing better than to have a good set, and having made them ourselves, we can sell them cheaper than the stores, and still make money on them."

"Say, that's a pretty good stunt," said Joe. "I was trying to figure out the other day where we could get the necessary cash. The cheapest audion bulb you can buy costs about three dollars."

The other boys, also, were pleased with this idea, and said so. They agreed to sell two of their sets as soon as they got back to Clintonia. This was their last week at Ocean Point, for the fall term of the high school started the following Monday, and they were to leave Ocean Point on Saturday.

"It will be pretty hard to bone down to lessons again, after a summer like this, but I suppose there's no help for it," said Jimmy, mournfully. "I feel as though I'd forgotten all I ever knew."

21

"That isn't much, so you don't need to worry about it," said Joe, with pleasing frankness.

"I suppose you think you're a regular Solomon, don't you?" retorted Jimmy. "Nobody else does, though, I can tell you that."

"Quit your scrapping," admonished Herb. "You don't either of you know a single good joke, while I'm just full of wit and humor. Why, here's a joke I thought up just the other day, and I don't mind admitting that it's a pippin, not to say peacherino. I thought it up while I was watching some fellows play tennis, and I just know you're all crazy to hear it."

"We'd have to be crazy to want to hear it," said Bob. "But probably you'll feel better after you get it out of your system, so fire ahead, and we'll do our best to stand the strain."

"This won't be any strain; it will be a pleasure," said Herb. "Now, this joke is in the form of a humorous question and an even more humorous answer. Oh, it's a wonder, I'll say."

"We'll say something, too, if you don't hurry up and get the agony over with," threatened Joe. "Make it snappy, before we weaken under the strain and throw you out the window."

"Well, then," said Herb: "Why does the tennis ball? And the answer is: Because the catgut on the racquet." And he broke into a peal of laughter, in which, however, his friends refused to join.

"Well, what's the matter?" asked Herb, cutting short his laughter as he saw that the others only shook their heads despondently. "Why in the name of all that's good don't you laugh? Wasn't that a peach of a joke?"

"Herb, the only reason we don't kill you right away is because you will be punished more by being allowed to live and suffer," said Bob. "That was a fierce joke."

"Oh, get out!" exclaimed Herb, in an injured tone. "You fellows don't know a clever joke when you hear it."

"Likely enough we don't," admitted Joe. "We don't get much chance to hear clever jokes while you're around."

"Oh, well, if you don't like my jokes, why don't you think up some of your own?" asked Herb, in an aggrieved tone. "There's no law against it, you know."

"There ought to be, though," put in Jimmy.

"Oh, what do you know about it?" asked Herb, incensed at the laughter that followed this thrust. "All you can think of, Doughnuts, is what you're going to get to eat when the next meal time comes around."

"Well, I enjoy thinking of that so much, that I'd be foolish to think of anything else," said Jimmy, serenely.

"You win, Jimmy," said Bob, as he and Joe shouted with laughter at Herb's discomfiture. The latter was inclined to be sulky at first, but he soon forgot his ill humor, and was as gay as the others as they discussed their plans for the fall and winter months.

Contrary to the predictions of some of their neighbors in Clintonia, their enthusiasm for radio work had increased rather than diminished, and they were anxious to become the possessors of sets capable of hearing any station in the United States, and perhaps even the large foreign stations. Of course, this meant that their apparatus would have to be much more intricate and expensive than any they had constructed hitherto, but the realization of this did not deter them. On the contrary, the thought that the task would be one to tax their skill and knowledge to the utmost only served to make them more eager to begin. They examined numberless catalogues and circulars in an effort to determine where and at what cost they could obtain their necessary supplies, jotting down notes as they went along. By supper time they had acquired a pretty good idea of what their new equipment would cost, and were pleased to find that it came within the amount that they thought they could get by selling two of their present complete sets.

"Well, then," said Bob, in conclusion, as they heard the supper bell ring, "the first thing we do when we get back home will be to sell the two sets, and then we'll get busy on making the new ones."

With this the others agreed.

CHAPTER V

BACK FROM THE BEACH

"Good-bye, old bungalows, we hate to leave you. Here's hoping we see you again next summer."

It was Herb speaking, as the radio boys and their families left the group of cottages where all had spent such an eventful and pleasant summer. Brilliant sunlight beat down on the yellow sand, but its heat was very different from the torrid rays that had kept them running to the ocean to cool off all that summer. There was a clear and sparkling appearance to the air and sky, and the wind that came sweeping over the level sands had a nip in it that made even Jimmy walk fast to keep warm.

They were to return home by train instead of automobile, and all the ladies had gone to the station in the big motor omnibus, but the boys had preferred to walk, as the distance was not great and there was still plenty of time before the train was due.

"We've had a wonderful time here, there's no doubt of that," said Bob, commenting on Herb's apostrophe to the bungalows. "But it will seem nice to get home again, too. I've almost forgotten what the old town looks like."

"It will seem good to see the old bunch at High once more, too," added Joe. "I'll bet there aren't many of them have had the fun that we've had ever since we landed at Ocean Point."

"Not only that, but we've learned a lot, too," said Bob. "We were running in luck when we met Mr. Harvey and had the run of that big station. It was a wonderful opportunity."

"You bet it was," agreed Herb. "It's a wonderful place to think up jokes in, too. I don't think I ever thought of so many good ones in a single summer before."

"I didn't know you thought of any good ones," said Joe. "All those that we heard were punk. Why didn't you tell us some of the good ones for a change?"

"So I did, you poor boob," retorted Herb. "My one regret here was that we didn't have a sending set. Then I could have broadcasted some of those jokes, and everybody could have had the benefit of them free of charge."

"It would have to be free of charge," said Jimmy, cruelly. "You don't suppose anybody would pay real money to hear that low brand of humor, do you?"

"Chances are they'd pay real money *not* to hear them," put in Joe, before Herb could answer. "But I suppose if Herb ever started anything like that the Government would take away his license before he could do much harm."

"Never mind," said Herb resignedly. "You can knock all you want now, but when I get to be rich and famous, like Mark Twain, for instance, you'll be sorry that you were so dumb that you couldn't appreciate me sooner."

"Well, we won't have to worry until you are rich and famous, and that probably won't be for a year or two yet," said Bob. "But here we are at the station. They all look glad to see us. I'll bet they were afraid we wouldn't get here in time."

This was indeed the case, as was evidenced by much gesturing and waving of parasols and handkerchiefs by the feminine members of the party. They had heard the whistle of the train in the distance, and had firmly persuaded themselves that the boys would be delayed and lose the train. As it turned out, however, the boys had plenty of time, and were on the platform and waiting as the engine puffed into the station.

As the train pulled out, they all gazed back regretfully at the little village that had become so familiar to them. Many of the shops were closed and shuttered for the season, and the main street wore a deserted air. However, as the train rounded a curve and the village was lost to view, they regained their usual spirits.

"It's a wonder you boys didn't miss the train altogether," said Agnes, Herb's sister. "I don't see why you didn't hurry a little. We were on pins and needles all the time until you showed up."

"Aw, what's the use of standing on an old station platform for an hour and spending your time wondering why the train doesn't show up?" said Herb. "We could have left the bungalows ten minutes later and still caught the train. I don't enjoy riding on a train unless I've had to run to get it, anyway."

"If this train had been on time, you would have had a fast run to get it, I can tell you," said Amy, Agnes' younger sister. "It was about fifteen minutes late, and that's the only reason you got it at all."

"Oh, we could run almost as fast as this train goes, anyway," boasted her brother. "And speaking of slow trains, that reminds me of a good story I read the other day."

"Oh, please tell us about it," said Agnes, with mock enthusiasm. "You know we always love to hear your jokes, brother dear."

Herb glanced suspiciously at her, but was too glad of an opportunity to tell his story to inquire into her sincerity.

"It seems there was a man traveling on a southern railroad——" he began, but Jimmy interrupted him.

"Which railroad?" he inquired.

"It doesn't matter which railroad," said Herb, glaring at his friend. "It was a railroad, anyway, and a slow one, too. Well, this man was in a hurry, it seems, and kept fidgeting around and looking at his watch. Finally the train stopped altogether, and a moment later the conductor came through the car.

"'What's the matter, Conductor?' asked the traveler.

"'There's a cow on the track,' answered the conductor.

"Well, pretty soon the train started on again, but it hadn't gone very far before it stopped once more. 'Say, Conductor, why in blazes have we stopped again?' asked the traveler. 'Seems to me this is the slowest train I ever rode on.'

"'It can't be helped, sir,' answered the conductor. 'We've caught up with that pesky cow again.'"

They all laughed at this anecdote, which pleased Herb immensely.

"I know lots more, any time you want to hear them," he ventured, hopefully.

"Better not take a chance on spoiling that one, Herb," advised Joe. "That was unusually good for you, I must admit."

"Herb's jokes wouldn't be so bad if he'd stick to regular ones," said Bob. "It's only when he starts making them up himself that they get so terrible."

"Yes, and just think of his poor sisters," sighed Agnes. "In the summer it isn't quite so bad, because he's out of the house most of the time, but in winter it's simply terrible."

"Well, this winter I won't have much time to waste on you and Amy, trying to develop a sense of humor in you," said Herb. "I'm going to build a radio set of my own that will be a cuckoo."

"Hurrah for you!" exclaimed Bob. "That's a better way to spend your time, and what a relief it will be for all of us."

"I suppose you think you're kidding me, but you're not," said Herbert. "I'll make a set this winter that will make you amateurs turn green with envy. You see if I don't!"

"It will be fine if you do," said Bob. "There's no reason why you shouldn't if you really want to."

The time passed quickly, and before they realized it they heard the conductor call the name of their own town.

25

"Goodness gracious!" exclaimed Agnes, "are we really there so soon? And I haven't got any of my things together yet!"

There was great bustle and confusion for a few moments, and then the whole party found themselves on the familiar platform of the Clintonia station. Several taxicabs were requisitioned, and they were all whisked away to their respective homes, after the radio boys had agreed to meet at Bob's house that evening.

CHAPTER VI

RADIO'S LONG ARM

"Well, fellows," said Bob, when they were together that evening, according to agreement, "this is the last evening we'll have without lessons for some time to come, so we'd better make the most of it."

"Don't mention lessons, Bob," implored Jimmy. "Oh, my, how I hate 'em!" and he groaned dismally.

"You'll soon be doing them, old timer, whether you like them or not," said Joe. "It's going to be a tough term for me, too. I'll be taking up geometry this term, and they say that's no cinch."

"Nothing's a cinch for me, worse luck," said Jimmy, dolefully. "Everything I do seems to be hard work for me."

"That's tough luck, too," said Bob, gravely, "because you hate work so much, Doughnuts."

"There isn't anybody in the world hates it more," confessed Jimmy, shamelessly. "But that's all the good it ever does me. Why wasn't I born rich instead of good looking?"

"Give it up," said Bob. "You'll have to ask me easier ones than that, Jimmy, if you expect to get an answer. But as far as I can see, people that are rich don't seem to be especially happy, anyway. Look at old Abubus Boggs. He's probably the richest man in Clintonia, but nobody ever accused him of being happy."

"I should say not!" exclaimed Joe. "He goes around looking as though he had just bitten into an especially sour lemon. Everybody hates him, and I don't suppose that makes any one happy."

"Maybe that does make old Abubus happy, there's no telling," said Jimmy, reflectively. "But I know I wouldn't change places for all his money."

"There you are!" exclaimed Bob, triumphantly. "You don't realize how well off you are, Doughnuts."

"Maybe not," conceded Jimmy. "School isn't so bad after you once get started, but I hate to think of settling down to the old grind after that wonderful summer at Ocean Point."

"But we'll have the radio just the same," Joe pointed out. "That's one of the good things about it; you can take it with you wherever you go."

"Yes, I was reading an article in one of the radio magazines a little while ago about that," said Bob. "The article was written by a trapper in the northern part of Canada. He told how he had set up his outfit in the center of a howling wilderness and had received all the latest news of the world in his shack, not to mention music of every kind. He said that the natives and Indians thought it must be magic, and were looking all over the shack for the spirit that they supposed must be talking into the headphones. That trapper was certainly a radio fan, if there ever was one, and he wrote a mighty interesting letter, too."

"I should think it would be interesting," said Herb. "I'd like to read it, if you still have it around."

Bob rummaged around in a big pile of radio magazines and finally found what he was looking for. The boys read every word of the letter, and were more than ever impressed by the wonderful possibilities of radiophony.

No longer would it be necessary for an exploring expedition to be lost sight of for months, or even years. Wedged in the Arctic ice floes, or contending with fever and savage animals in the depths of some tropical jungle, the explorers could keep in touch with the civilized world as easily as though bound on a week end fishing trip. The aeroplane soaring in the clouds far above the earth, or the submarine under the earth's waters, could be informed and guided by it. Certainly of all the wonders of modern times, this was the most marvelous and far-reaching.

Something of all this passed through the boys' minds as they sat in ruminative silence, thinking of the lonely man in the wilderness with his precious wireless.

"I suppose we should feel pretty lucky to be around just at this stage of the earth's history," said Bob, thoughtfully. "We're living in an age of wonders, and I suppose we're so used to them that most of the time we don't realize how wonderful they really are."

"That's true enough, all right," agreed Joe. "When you step into an automobile these days, you don't stop to think that a few years ago the fastest way to travel was behind old Dobbin. The old world is stepping ahead pretty lively these days, and no mistake."

"It can't step too fast to suit me," said Herb. "Speed is what I like to see, every time."

"Oh, I don't know," said Jimmy, lazily. "Why not take things a little easier. People had just as much fun out of life when they weren't in such a rush about everything. I take things easy and get fat on it, while Herb is always rushing around, and it wears him down until he has the same general appearance as a five and ten cent store clothespin."

"I wouldn't want to look like a three and nine cent store pin-cushion, anyway," said Herb, indignantly. "That's about your style of beauty, Doughnuts."

"Well, I never expect to take any prizes in a beauty show, so that doesn't make me mad," said Jimmy, calmly.

"If you weren't so blamed fat, I'd have half a mind to throw you out the window, you old faker," said Herb, threateningly.

"Couldn't do it," said Jimmy, briefly. "In the first place, I'm too heavy; and in the second place, Bob wouldn't let you."

"I'll bet Bob would be glad to see you thrown out. How about it, Bob?" and Herb appealed to his friend.

"I wouldn't want you to throw him out of either of these windows," answered Bob, seriously. "There are valuable plants on the lawn below, and I'd hate to see them damaged. But if you want to take him out and drop him from the hall window, I'm sure nobody will have any objections."

"Oh, I can't be bothered carrying him that far," said Herb. "Guess I might as well let him live a while longer, after all."

"That's very nice of you," said Jimmy, sarcastically. "But you know you couldn't do it, anyway. All I'd have to do would be to fall on you, Herb, and it would be curtains for little Herbert."

"I think they're both afraid of each other, Joe," said Bob, turning to his friend. "What's your opinion?"

"Looks that way to me, too. They remind me of a couple of cats that stand and yell at each other for an hour, and then walk off without mixing it after all."

"Well, we're not going to go to mauling each other just to amuse you two Indians, that's certain," said Herb. "Let's shake hands and show the world we're friends, Jimmy."

"Righto!" agreed his good-natured friend, and they laughingly shook hands.

"We'd better save our scrapping for Buck Looker and his friends," said Bob. "I suppose they'll be up to some kind of mischief as soon as we get back to school again. They seem never to learn by experience."

"They're too foolish and conceited to learn much," observed Joe. "They probably think they know all there is to know already."

"In spite of that, we may be able to teach them a trick or two," said Herb. "But whether you fellows know it or not, it's getting pretty late, so I think I'll go and hit the hay. Who's coming my way?"

"I suppose we might as well all beat it," returned Joe, rising. "If we don't see each other to-morrow, I suppose we'll all meet at the dear old high school on Monday morning. Three silent cheers, fellows."

"Consider them given," laughed Bob. "But we'll have plenty of fun, too, so why mind a little hard work?"

After hunting in odd corners for their caps, the boys finally found them all and departed gayly on their way, only slightly depressed by the imminence of the fall term at high school.

CHAPTER VII

LEARNING TO SEND

"I've got two customers for those sets we wanted to sell," announced Bob, a few evenings later, when the radio boys had congregated at his house as usual. "It was so easy, that I'll bet we could sell all we make, if we wanted to."

"Who's going to buy them?" asked Joe.

"Dave Halley, who runs the barber shop near the station, wants one, and there's a big novelty store on the next block whose owner will take the other. I promised that we'd set the outfits up and show them how to work them."

"That's quick work, Bob," laughed Herb. "How did you come to land two customers so quickly?"

"I was getting a haircut in Dave's shop, and he told me that he was thinking of buying a good set, but hated to spend the money. So I told him that I could sell him a good practical set for quite a little less than it would cost him in a store, and he jumped at the offer. Then he told me about Hartmann, the owner of the new variety store. Hartmann wants to get one because he thinks it will draw trade. I went to see him as soon as Dave got through telling me how much dandruff I had and how much I needed some of his patent tonic. Mr. Hartmann was a little doubtful at first about buying a home made set, but I told him if he wasn't pleased with it he didn't need to pay us for it and we'd take it back. That seemed to satisfy him, so he said he'd buy it. It was dead easy."

"Well, that's certainly fine," said Joe, admiringly. "That will help a lot toward getting apparatus for the new sets."

"You're a hustler, Bob," said Jimmy. "I'd like to be one, but I guess I'm not built that way."

"It was more luck than anything else," disclaimed Bob. "Let's go down to the store after school to-morrow and pick out what we need. I want a couple of audion bulbs, and I suppose you fellows do, too. I want to price variable condensers like the one Doctor Dale brought us at Ocean Point last summer, too."

"We've got to keep busy if we want to keep ahead of some of the other fellows in this town," said Joe. "Lots of the fellows at High have got the radio fever bad, and are out to beat us at our own game. I guess we can show them where they get off, all right, but we may have to hustle some to do it. I heard Lon Beardsley at noon to-day boasting that he was going to be the first fellow in Clintonia to receive signals from Europe. I asked him what kind of set he intended to do it with, and he said he had been working on one all summer, and was putting the finishing touches to it now."

"He ought to have something pretty good, if he's been working on it that long," commented Herb. "If one of us had been working on a set all summer, I think we'd have had it done before this."

"Probably we would. But you've got to remember that we've had more experience at the game than Lon," Bob reminded him.

"It seems to me that we'd do better all to work on one big, crackerjack set than each to make a separate long distance set," said Herb. "In the first place, it's more fun working together. And then we could put our money together and get better equipment than we could the other way. What do you think?"

"I think it's a pretty good idea," said Jimmy. "You can hear just as much over one set as you can over four, as far as that goes."

"I was thinking of something like that myself," said Bob, slowly. "It would certainly cost us less, and, as Herb says, we'd probably have a better set in the end."

"It suits me all right," added Joe. "This is going to be a tough term at High, and with so much home work I don't know where I'd get the time to build a complicated set. It looks as though we'd be better off every way, doesn't it?"

"You always will be better off, if you follow my advice," said Herb, with his customary modesty. "You don't usually have sense enough to do it, though."

"We have too much sense, you mean," said Jimmy, scornfully. "This suggestion of yours was only an accident, Herb. Chances are you won't make another as good for the next year."

"I don't know that you're very famous for bright ideas, Jimmy, so where do you get off to criticize?" asked Herb.

"Huh! I've got an idea in my noddle right now that's worth half a dozen of yours."

"Prove it!" replied Herb, promptly. "What is this bright idea?"

"Well, you know that just about this time they cook nice, hot doughnuts down at Mattatuck's bakery. Delicious doughnuts! Um, yum!" and Jimmy's round countenance assumed a rapturous expression.

"And the idea was, that you'd go down there and blow the crowd to hot doughnuts, was it?" queried Joe.

"Blow, nothing!" exclaimed Jimmy. "We'll all chip in. But I don't mind going after them."

"The trouble is—can we trust you not to eat them all on the way back?" Bob laughed.

"Anybody that doesn't think so can go for his own doughnuts," replied Jimmy. "Kick in there, you hobos, and I'll be on my way. I'm getting hungrier every minute."

His friends, thus adjured, "kicked in," and Jimmy set off at a rate of speed much above his usual leisurely gait. The bakery was three or four blocks away, but Jimmy returned in a surprisingly short time with a large bag of tender doughnuts, still warm from the bakery.

"Wow!" exclaimed Joe, as Jimmy tore open the bag. "The sight of those doughnuts certainly makes a fellow feel hungry."

"Dig into them, fellows," was Jimmy's only comment, as he reached for one himself.

They all followed this example, and the pile of crisp brown doughnuts dwindled with surprising rapidity.

"Likely enough these will keep me awake half the night, but it's worth it," said Jimmy, with a sigh of contentment, as he finished the last crumb of his fourth doughnut. "I don't feel near as hungry as I did, anyway."

"I should hope that you didn't feel hungry at all, old greedy," laughed Joe. "I'm beginning to think that it's impossible to fill you up any more."

"Oh, lay off!" retorted Jimmy. "You Indians ate your full share, I notice."

"I guess we're all in the same boat," agreed Bob. "But now that we're fed up and feeling strong, how would you like to practice sending for awhile? I was just beginning to work up a little speed while we were at Ocean Point, but now I suppose I'm getting rusty again. Who's game to send? I'll bet nobody can send faster than I can receive."

"I'm willing to try it, anyway," said Joe, picking up a magazine. "I'll send right out of this magazine, so when you say 'stop' we'll be able to check up how much you've caught."

"All right, that's fair enough," agreed Bob. "Just wait a minute until I get a paper and pencil, then shoot as fast as you can."

Seating himself at the table, with a blank sheet of paper before him, Bob made ready to scribble at high speed, while Herb held a watch to time him. As for Jimmy, he was content to curl up on a sofa and act the part of self-appointed judge.

"Start sending as soon as you like, Joe," said, Jimmy. "I'm all ready for you. I'll bet I can fall asleep before you can send fifty words."

"I wouldn't take that bet, because I believe you can," replied Joe. "I'd be betting against your specialty, and there's no percentage in that, you know."

"Don't forget me, though, will you?" said Bob, in a resigned tone. "I don't want to hurry you, but any time you're both through that interesting conversation I'm waiting to begin."

"All right, then, here goes!" said Joe, and started sending as rapidly as he could with the practice key and buzzer.

Bob's pencil fairly flew over the paper, and for five minutes there was no sound in the room save the strident buzz of the sender and the whisper of Bob's pencil as it moved rapidly over the paper.

Then, "Time," called Herb, and Bob threw down the pencil.

"Whew!" he exclaimed, reaching for a handkerchief. "That's pretty hot work, if any one should ask you. Count 'em up, Herb, will you, and see how many there are? Seems to me there must be a million words there, more or less."

"Quite a little less," laughed Herb, after he had counted the words as requested. "But you've written ninety-one, which is mighty good."

"That's a little over sixteen a minute," said Bob. "It's not near as fast as I want to get, but it's fast enough to get a license, anyway."

"You bet it is!" exclaimed Herb. "And there are very few mistakes," he added, as he compared what Bob had written with the magazine text.

"Joe's getting to be some bear at sending, too," remarked Bob.

"Oh, the sending is a lot easier than receiving," said Joe. "But now, if you don't mind, Bob, you can send me something, and I'll see how fast I can take it. I'm afraid I can't come up to your record, though."

Joe did very well, however, averaging about fourteen words a minute.

Then Herb took a turn at sending and receiving, as did Jimmy, and they both did well. The boys found it all very fascinating, as well as useful, and discussed many plans for the future, although they did not intend to go in much for sending until they had perfected a first-class receiving set. They agreed before parting for the night that they would meet the following day after school at the radio supply store, where they could buy some audion bulbs and whatever other apparatus they might need.

CHAPTER VIII

A RATTLING FIGHT

"Hello, Bob! what kept you so late?" called Joe. He and Herb and Jimmy had been waiting some time for their friend, and were beginning to think that he must have forgotten the appointment made the previous night.

"It's a wonder I got here as soon as I did," replied Bob. His face was flushed, and there was an angry gleam in his eyes. "I thought I'd have to lick Carl Lutz before I could get here; but he didn't have quite nerve enough to start anything, as he was all alone. I only wish he had."

"What happened?" asked Joe. "Tell us about it."

"When I came out this afternoon, Carl was standing just outside the schoolyard gate, teasing that little Yates kid, whose brother was killed in the Argonne fighting. If Bill had been alive, you can bet Carl would have left the kid brother alone, but as it was, he was bullying him and trying to make him carry a big package for him."

"Just like the big coward!" exclaimed Joe, indignantly.

"You said it!" replied Bob. "Well, of course, I wasn't going to stand for anything like that, and I made him quit. He got so mad that I really thought he was going to swing at me, but he didn't quite have the nerve. He went off muttering something about getting the gang after me, and I took the Yates kid with me for a few blocks to make sure that he would get home all right."

"Good for you!" said Joe. "That's just like Carl, to pick on a kid that has nobody to fight his battles for him and is too small to fight his own. I'm glad you were around to take the kid's part."

"I suppose Carl will run right to Buck, now, and they'll hatch up some scheme to get even with you," remarked Herb.

"I don't care what they do," returned Bob. "It's too bad there's a bunch like that in this town. They're a regular nuisance."

"We've done all we could to teach them manners," said Joe. "I guess the trouble is, they don't want to learn."

"Don't let's bother even thinking about them," said Bob. "Come on in and we'll buy the stuff we need."

The four friends went on into the store, where they found several of their schoolmates, bent on the same mission as themselves. All exchanged greetings, and many good-natured jokes were bandied back and forth as they made their purchases.

"You fellows will have to step lively to get ahead of me," said Lon Beardsley, who was older than any of the radio boys and was in the senior class at High School. He was one of the brightest boys in his class, and the others knew that competition from him was not to be despised.

"Stepping fast is one of the best things we do," said, Bob, in answer to this friendly challenge. "You may be some speed, but we're not such slouches, either."

"Do your worst! We defy you!" cried Herb, striking a melodramatic attitude.

"All right," said Lon, laughing. "Remember, though, I've given you fair warning. I see you're buying vacuum tubes," he added, curiously. "You must be going in pretty deep, aren't you?"

"Ask us no questions and we'll tell you no lies," parried Bob. "Besides, we're not the only radio fans in this town, Lon. Maybe some one else will beat us all out."

"Oh, I'm not worrying," said the other, as he prepared to leave with his purchases. "Are you fellows going my way?"

"You'd better not wait for us," replied Bob. "We've got a few things to get yet. See you at school to-morrow."

"Righto!" said Lon, and departed, whistling cheerfully.

The radio boys started home soon afterward, The days were getting very short, and by the time they left the store the autumn evening was rapidly fading into night. There was a crisp tang in the air which, together with the smell of burning leaves, gave warning that winter was close at hand. The last gorgeous colors of an autumn sunset still tinged the western rim of the sky as the boys set out for home at a rapid pace.

Not far from their homes they struck off from the street through a vacant lot, following a path that served as a short cut. The lot was overgrown with weeds and high sunflower stalks, but the idea of an ambush never entered the boys' heads until suddenly they were assailed by a shower of stones, which sang viciously past their ears. Fortunately, it was too dark for their assailants to throw the missiles with any accuracy, although the boys were struck more than once.

For a moment, taken completely by surprise, they did not know which way to turn nor what to do. But they were not of the type that hesitates long before taking action. Their hidden assailants probably thought that they would run, but this thought was furthest from their minds.

Bob noted from which direction the missiles were coming, and acted accordingly.

"Come on, fellows!" he yelled, and, followed by his friends, charged into the long dry stalks that fringed the path.

There was a sudden cessation in the volley of stones and a startled rustling deep in the rank growth of weeds.

In grim silence the radio boys charged straight in the direction of this sound, and such was the speed of their attack that their hidden adversaries had no chance to make their escape before the boys were upon them. It was now almost dark, but there was still enough light for the boys to recognize the ungainly form of Buck Looker, in company with his cronies. These three had been re-inforced by a boy of about Buck's age, and of very much the same ugly disposition, known as Bud Hayes, whose family had lately moved to Clintonia.

"Clean them up, fellows!" yelled Bob. "We'll teach them not to throw stones again in a hurry!"

Each of the radio boys singled out an adversary, and a brisk mêlée ensued. Seeing that they could not get away, the Looker crowd put up the best fight they could. But the radio boys were wrought up to a high pitch of anger by the cowardly attack on them, and they fought with a quiet and grim determination that quickly put their adversaries on the defensive.

At first the high grass and weeds hampered all the combatants, but these were soon trampled down as they fought savagely back and forth. Suddenly, by some unfortunate accident, Herb tripped over some object lying on the ground, and fell full length. With a cry of triumph, Bud Hayes, without giving Herb a chance to get to his feet again, threw himself down on top of him and started pommeling him for all he was worth. Stunned by his fall, Herb at first could offer little resistance, and it would have gone hard with him had not Bob observed his fall. He himself had engaged Buck in combat, but as he saw Herb go down, he dealt Buck a staggering blow on the point of the jaw and leaped to Herb's assistance.

Hot rage filled his heart and the wild thrill of combat tingled along every nerve. With the strength and ferocity of a panther he hurled himself at Bud Hayes, landing with such force that Bud was hurled several feet away from the prostrate Herb, gasping for breath.

Bob himself landed on the ground, but was on his feet again quick as lightning, glancing about him to see how it fared with his friends. Joe was forcing Carl Lutz back step by step, while Jimmy had already forced Terry Mooney to take to his heels. But even as Bob noted this in one quick glance, both Bud and Buck, who had recovered by this time, rushed at him from different directions. But before Buck could get too close quarters Herb, who was recovering from the effect of his fall, stretched out a foot, and Buck sprawled headlong, landing with such force that the breath was knocked from his body.

Lutz and Hayes, seeing their leader fall, decided that it was time for them to get away, and simultaneously they took to their heels. By this time it had grown so dark that it was impossible to follow them, so the boys were left in undisputed possession of the field.

Buck Looker, deserted by his cowardly friends, staggered to his feet, all the fight knocked out of him. He was entirely at the mercy of the radio boys, but

34

they were not the kind to take advantage of this fact, although, undoubtedly, had their positions been reversed, Buck would have had no such scruples.

"Well, you've got me," growled Buck. "What are you going to do about it?"

"Nothing," said Bob, a note of contempt in his voice. "The less we see of you, Buck, the better we're satisfied. And your gang's no better than you are. Look at the way they ran off and left you to take care of yourself. You're dirty and they're dirty. We'll let you off this time with the licking you've had already, but if you ever try any more low-down tricks you won't get off so easily."

Buck muttered something to himself which he did not dare to voice aloud, and slunk off with the manner of a cur who has just received a beating that he knows he deserves. The radio boys groped their way back to the path, where they had left their bundles, and resumed their way home, keeping a wary eye out for any signs of a renewal of the attack by their enemies.

CHAPTER IX

LARRY REAPPEARS

"That was a regular battle," said Herb, as they walked along. "Bud Hayes has some reputation as a scrapper, and he certainly was all that I could handle, but if I hadn't tripped over that blamed can I could have taken care of him all right. But I've got a lump on my head as big as a hen's egg where I hit the ground."

"You'd have been out of luck if Bob hadn't helped you out the way he did," said Joe. "You certainly landed on him like a load of bricks, Bob."

"I was so mad that I think I would have dropped a ton of bricks on him if I'd had them handy," replied Bob, with a grim laugh. "That was one dirty trick—hitting Herb—when he was knocked out by that fall."

"I guess I owe you a vote of thanks for that, too," said Herb.

"I owe you one, for tripping up Buck in the neat way you did," returned Bob. "He and Hayes would have been on top of me both together if you hadn't."

"No thanks due; it was a pleasure," grinned Herb, although a swollen lip made this exercise painful. "I wish he'd broken his neck while he was about it."

"It wasn't your fault that he didn't," said Bob.

"I knew that bunch was mean," remarked Joe. "But I never thought they were mean enough to take up stone throwing from ambush. That's the most cowardly thing they've ever done."

"Yes, and the most dangerous," said Bob. "Any one of those stones might have killed one of us if it had landed just right."

"Or, worse still, it might have broken our vacuum tubes," added Jimmy, with a grin. "It's a wonder that the whole lot of them didn't get smashed. I'll be afraid to open the package when we do get it home," he went on more seriously.

His fears turned out to have been groundless, for when they arrived at the Layton home, without having seen or heard anything more of the bullies on the way, they found all their delicate apparatus unharmed. And other than Herb's swollen lip and a few slight bruises, they had received little damage themselves from the encounter. The bullies had not fared so well, for little was seen of them for several days, and when they did make an appearance in public they were decorated with strips of court plaster here and there. They offered many ingenious excuses in explanation, but they received little credence from the other boys of the town, who had been apprized of the cowardly attack on the radio boys and the result of the encounter.

The bullies soon found that nobody believed them, and wherever they went they were pointed out and were the subject of many jeers and jokes, although few dared to make them openly. Buck realized that he was losing prestige rapidly, and, although he was getting secretly to fear another encounter with the radio boys, he felt that he must soon get the better of them if he were to regain his former reputation as a fighter. He and his cronies spent many an hour in hatching plots against Bob and his friends, but for a long time could think of nothing that offered much prospect of success.

Meanwhile, the radio boys were going about the building of their big set with enthusiasm, spending all their spare time at the fascinating pursuit. Most of their work was done at Bob's house, as he had an ideal workroom in the cellar, and his position as leader, moreover, made it seem the natural place for them to meet.

"Say, fellows!" exclaimed Jimmy one evening, tumbling down the cellar stairs three steps at a time, "have you heard the news?"

"What news?" asked Herb, who had arrived only a few minutes before him. "Has there been a big fire? Or did some one die and leave you a million dollars?"

"No such luck as that," replied Jimmy. "But I know you'll be mighty glad to hear it, anyway. Chasson's vaudeville is going to be in Clintonia next week. That's the show Larry and Tim are with, you know."

"Good enough!" exclaimed the others. "Where did you hear about it, Jimmy?" asked Bob.

"There was a bill poster putting up the programme on a fence as I came along," answered Jimmy. "I saw the name 'Chasson,' and of course I stopped and looked to see if Larry and Tim were on the bill."

"Were they?" asked Herb.

"You bet they were! And in pretty big type, too," responded Jimmy. "Say! it will be great to see them on the stage, won't it?"

"I should say it will," said Joe. "If they're half as funny on the stage as they are off it, they'll surely make a hit."

"They certainly will," put in Bob. "We'll be there on the opening night to give them a hand. If they don't go big, it won't be our fault."

"They'll be popular, all right," predicted Joe, with conviction. "If the rest of the show is half as good as their part it will be worth more than the price of admission."

"It will be great to hear that canary whistling his little tunes again," said Herbert, laughing at the recollection of Larry's comical imitations.

"Not to mention Tim's dancing," said Bob. "That boy can sure shake a foot. I'll bet they'll both get into the big circuits before they're much older."

"They deserve to," said Jimmy. "They rehearse an awful lot. It makes me tired just to think of how hard I've seen them work sometimes."

"But then, you get tired very easily, Doughnuts, you know that," said Joe.

"If you worked half as hard in the afternoons as I do sometimes, you'd be tired in the evening, too," replied Jimmy, in an injured tone. "I'll bet I sawed through about a thousand feet of tough oak planking this afternoon for Dad, and I'll have to do the same thing to-morrow afternoon. He's got a big job on, and I have to pitch in and help him."

"Well, you ought to do something to pay for all the good grub you pack away," said Herb, utterly without sympathy for his friend's tale of woe.

"Maybe you'd pack away more if you did a little work once in a while," retorted Jimmy. "All you do is spend your time thinking up poor jokes instead of doing something useful."

"Oh, I'm glad you mentioned jokes," said Herb, calmly ignoring Jimmy's attack. "I thought of a swell one just as I was walking up here this evening. I know you will all be delighted to hear it."

"What makes you so sure?" asked Bob. "They don't usually delight anybody, do they?"

"Of course they do," replied Herb, indignantly.

"They always delight Herb Fennington, anyway," observed Joe.

"Yes, I like me," said Herb, refusing to get mad. "Also, I like my jokes. Now, take this one, for instance. Why——"

"I'd rather not take it, if it's all the same to you," said Joe, cruelly. "Why don't you keep it, and give it to somebody else, Herb?"

"Oh, forget it!" exclaimed Herb. "This is a good joke, I tell you, and you've got to listen, whether you want to or not."

"Go ahead and get the agony over with, then," said Bob, resignedly. "I suppose we'll be able to live through it, just as we have others before this."

"Well, I saw in this morning's newspaper that the Mercury Athletic Club in New York burned up last night. Now, you've got to help me out with this joke, Bob. When I say 'I see there was a big athletic event at the Mercury Athletic Club last night,' you say 'is that so? What happened?' Have you got that through your noddle?"

"Yes, I guess I can remember that," answered Bob. "Shoot!"

"All right, then, here goes," said Herb. "I see that there was a big athletic event at the Mercury Athletic Club last night, Bob."

"Is that so?" said Bob, taking his cue. "What happened, Herb?"

"The water was running and the flames were leaping," cried Herb, triumphantly. "How's that for a crackerjack joke?"

"Awful," said Joe, although he could not help laughing with the others. "I'll bet there's a nice cosy, padded cell waiting for you in the nearest bughouse, Herb."

"Well, it can wait, for all of me," said his friend. "I'm not very keen about it, myself."

"I think jail would be a better place for him," suggested Jimmy.

This met with the unqualified approval of everybody except Herb, and then the boys set to work on their new radio set. As this was Saturday evening, they had no lessons to prepare, and they worked steadily until ten o'clock. They wound transformers until Jimmy declared that it made him dizzy even to look at them, and when the time came to stop work they all felt that substantial progress had been made.

They agreed to meet at the theater the following Monday evening, to witness the opening performance of the show in which their friends Larry Bartlett and Tim Barcommon were performing, and then said good-night and started homeward to the accompaniment of a cheerful whistled marching tune.

There was much excitement among their classmates the following Monday, as they had all heard about the show and most of them intended to go. When they learned that the radio boys were acquainted with two of the performers, the four lads were deluged with questions as to how they came to know them.

"You fellows are getting pretty sporty, seems to me," said Lon Beardsley. "Maybe you'll give us an introduction to your friends in the show."

"Surest thing you know," assented Bob. "I got a letter from them this morning, and they promised to call me up around four o'clock this afternoon. They'll probably come to our house for dinner, and we'll all go down to the theater together."

And sure enough, Bob had hardly reached home that afternoon when the telephone bell rang, and Larry's familiar voice came over the wire.

"Hello, Bob!" he said. "How's the boy? Did you get my letter all right?"

"I sure did," answered Bob. "It's fine to hear your voice again. We're all tickled to death to know that you're showing in Clintonia this week. You and Tim have got to come here for supper to-night, you know."

"We'd be glad to, if it isn't imposing on your folks," said Larry. "We don't get many regular home dinners these days, you can bet, and it will be a treat for us."

"All right, then, we'll be looking for you," replied Bob. "Get here as early as you can."

This Larry promised to do, and after a little further conversation rang off. Bob then called up the other radio boys and told them to come to his house immediately after supper, so that they would have time for a few words with Larry and Tim, after which they could all go down to the theater together.

CHAPTER X

A TERRIBLE ACCIDENT

"Hello, Tim! Hello, Larry! How have you been?" The two actors had little reason to complain of the warmth of their reception, as the radio boys shook hands with them, pounded them on the back, and asked innumerable questions.

"You both look as though you were being treated all right," said Joe, after they had quieted down somewhat after the first riotous greetings. "How do you like being with a regular show?"

"Oh, we manage to get along," answered Larry. "But tell us a little of what you fellows have been doing since we saw you last. Are you still as interested in radio as ever?"

"You bet we are!" said Bob. "If you once get interested in that, I don't think you'd ever be willing to drop it. The more you learn about it, the more you want to learn."

"Well, that's fine," said Larry, heartily. "I only wish I had time enough to take it up. I'd like nothing better."

"When you make a lot of money in the vaudeville business and retire, you'll have plenty of time for it," said Tim, with a wink at the others.

"Yes, when I do," said Larry, scornfully. "It doesn't strain my back at present to carry around my roll, though. I feel lucky if I can keep a jump or two ahead of the wolf, as it is. But we may both have luck and land on a big circuit, and then we'll begin to get some real money."

While talking, the little party had been walking at a brisk pace and now found themselves close to the theater. Many of the townspeople were going in the same direction, and most of these recognized the radio boys and looked inquisitively at their two companions. Some of their schoolmates, who knew that Larry and Tim were actors, made bold to join the group and be introduced. By the time they reached the theater Larry and Tim had quite an escort of honor, all of whom were loath to leave them at the stage door. As they disappeared within they were followed by three rousing cheers, and then all the boys made their way to the main entrance.

The radio boys had secured their tickets in advance, and were soon comfortably seated, waiting expectantly for the curtain to rise on the first act.

This proved to be an acrobatic turn of mediocre quality, and the boys waited impatiently for it to finish, for Tim and Larry were billed to appear in the next act. With a moderate meed of applause, the acrobats retired. The orchestra struck up a catchy tune and the big curtain slowly rose. The scene disclosed was pretty and artistic, representing a glade in a forest, realistic trees surrounding a green clearing. Nothing was to be seen of Larry and Tim, however, and the radio boys were mystified, as both their friends had refused to tell them what the act was like. Suddenly the first piping notes of a canary bird's song were heard, rising so clear and lifelike that even the boys themselves were deluded at first into thinking that they were listening to an actual bird. The canary song ended with a sustained trill, and then, soft and melodious, came the limpid notes of the mocking bird's song. By this time the audience had comprehended that this was in reality a clever human imitation of bird notes, and they applauded heartily.

"Say!" whispered Jimmy, excitedly, "Larry has picked up a lot of new stuff since he was at Ocean Point. That was fine, wasn't it?"

"Keep still," whispered Joe, fiercely. "We want to hear every bit of this."

Jimmy subsided, and they all listened with keen delight as Larry imitated a host of feathered songsters, each one so true to life that the audience applauded again and again. At last Larry exhausted his repertoire, and for the first time appeared in the open, emerging from behind the trunk of a tree. He was heartily applauded, and as he bowed his way off the stage, the spotlight shifted, and Tim came onto the stage like a whirlwind, arms and legs flying as he did a complicated clog dance. At the most furious part Larry joined him, and they danced together, keeping such perfect time and going through such identical motions that it seemed as though they must be automatons actuated by the same string.

As a spectacular finale to the act, each one was supposed to make a dash for one of the property trees in the background, climb up it and disappear in the branches as the curtain fell. With a final wild gyration that brought spontaneous applause from the audience, each one made for his appointed tree, and started up.

Everything went as usual until Larry had almost reached the branches. Suddenly there came a cracking sound, the artificial tree swayed and tottered, and, amid horrified cries from the spectators, crashed to the stage, bringing down others on top of it as it fell. The radio boys had just time to see Larry lying, white and senseless, among the ruins when the curtain descended quickly, shutting off the scene of the accident from the audience.

So suddenly had the thing happened that at first the boys could hardly believe the evidence of their eyes. For a few moments they gazed at one another in horrified silence, and then, as though all were moved simultaneously by the same thought, they rushed down the aisle and, before the ushers could stop them, climbed onto the stage. It took them a few seconds, that seemed like hours, to find their way behind the scenes to the place where the accident had occurred.

Tim, aided by several stage hands, was frantically trying to release his partner from the heavy pieces of scenery that held him pinned down. Bob and his friends fell to the work of rescue with every ounce of energy and strength that they possessed, but, work as they did, it was a considerable time before they at last managed to free their unfortunate friend.

A doctor had been sent for, and by the time Larry was laid, still unconscious, on a cot, the physician had arrived. As he made his examination his face grew more and more serious, and he shook his head doubtfully.

"He's pretty badly hurt, I'm afraid," he said. "We must get him to a hospital as soon as possible. I have my car outside, and if some of you will carry him out, I'll take him there."

In sorrowful silence Tim and the radio boys carried their injured friend out to the doctor's automobile. Tim got in with him, and Larry was whirled away to the hospital, where he faced a grim fight for life.

The radio boys followed on foot, after first telephoning to their homes to explain why they would not be home until late.

Meantime, in the theater, the performance had gone on after an announcement by the management that "Mr. Bartlett is but slightly hurt,"—so spoke the manager—"and has been taken to a hospital where he can receive better care than in the hotel."

The radio boys followed the doctor's car to the hospital and spent an anxious hour in the waiting room while their friend was being thoroughly examined by the head physician, for of course the announcement at the theater had been made to quiet the audience, and no one yet knew just how serious Larry's injuries were.

"We'll have to get Doctor Ellis to take care of him," said Bob, while they were waiting. "I'm awfully sorry your father isn't in town, Joe. Next to him Dr. Ellis is the best doctor in Clintonia, I guess."

The others concurred in this view, and Bob promised to call up Dr. Ellis in the morning. After what seemed an endless wait the physician who had brought Larry to the hospital entered the waiting room.

"I'm afraid you won't be able to see your friend to-night," he said. "His left arm is broken, and I think his back is injured, although I can't tell yet how seriously. By this time to-morrow night I'll be able to tell you more. Has he any relatives that should be notified of the accident?"

"I know he has a mother, who is dependent on him," said Bob. "We've all heard him speak of her. I don't know where she lives, though, but probably Tim would have her address."

"Whose address?" asked Tim, entering the room at that moment.

"Larry's mother's," said Bob. "Do you know where she lives, Tim? As the doctor says, she ought to be notified about this."

"Yes, I know where she can be reached," said Tim. "I'll write to her before I go to bed to-night. Poor Larry!" and Tim tried hard to wink the tears back, but with little success.

"You mustn't feel too bad," advised the kindly doctor. "I think that there is little doubt that he will live, but as to whether or not he'll fully recover, I can't say yet. But we'll hope for the best, and you can rest assured that everything possible will be done for him."

The boys thanked the doctor for the help he had given their unfortunate friend, and then, after taking a sorrowful leave of Tim, started homeward.

The next few days were anxious ones for the radio boys. Larry hovered between life and death, and almost a week had passed before the doctors in charge of his case would say positively that he was going to pull through. At the end of that period the boys were allowed to see him, for a few minutes, after promising not to let him talk or to say anything to him that might excite him.

Larry received them with his old cheerful grin, but the boys were shocked at his wan and wasted appearance, so different from his usual vigorous self. They did not let him see this, however, but talked and joked with him in the usual way, and when the doctor finally signaled for them to leave they had the satisfaction of knowing that they had cheered their friend up and left him looking happier than when they came.

CHAPTER XI

LIGHT OUT OF DARKNESS

"It's going to be pretty hard for Larry when he does start to get around, I'm afraid," said Bob, after the boys had left the hospital. "Tim told me yesterday that Larry's mother is an invalid, and has to have a nurse all the time. Larry is her only support, and if he can't keep up his vaudeville career I don't see how either of them are going to get along."

"It's pretty tough, all right," replied Joe. "The doctor says now that he'll be as strong as ever eventually, but he admits that it will be a long time until he is. I wish we could think of some way to help Larry out until he gets on his feet again."

"Well, maybe we can," observed Bob, hopefully. "Although I must admit that I can't see much light on the subject just at present."

"We'll have to get busy on our new radio set in earnest pretty soon," said Joe, after a pause in which each had been busy with his own thoughts. "We've spent so much of our time at the hospital with Larry that we haven't got more than about ten cents' worth done since the night of the accident."

"We can plug right along with it now," said Bob. "And speaking of radio, who do you think called me up last night? I meant to tell you before, but I forgot all about it."

"Who was it?" asked Herb. "Somebody we all know?"

"You bet we all know him," said Bob, laughing. "It was Frank Brandon."

"Frank Brandon!" they all exclaimed. "Where's he been keeping himself lately?" asked Joe.

"He said that he had had to go to Florida on some government business connected with wireless, and he just got back to this part of the country yesterday," replied Bob. "He expected to be in Clintonia to-day, and said that if we were all going to be at my house to-night, he'd drop in and make us a visit."

"I hope you told him that we'd be there," said Jimmy.

"Of course I did," replied Bob. "You fellows had better get around bright and early this evening, because he said he'd be around right after supper. I know I've got plenty of questions I want to ask him, and I guess you have, too."

"You can bet I have!" exclaimed Jimmy. "I want to ask him where he got that package of milk chocolate he had with him the last time I saw him. He gave me a piece, and believe me, it was about the best I've ever tasted."

"There you go again," exclaimed Herb, with a laugh, "always thinking of that stomach of yours. Don't you ever think of anything serious?"

"Serious?" echoed Jimmy. "It's a serious enough thing for me, where to get that milk chocolate. I've been in pretty nearly every candy store in town, but none of them seems to have anything quite so good."

By this time the boys had reached Main Street, and they parted for the time being, promising to get to Bob's house as soon as they could after supper.

The Layton family had hardly finished their evening meal when there came a ring at the doorbell, and Bob jumped up to admit the expected guest.

"Hello, Mr. Brandon!" exclaimed Bob, as they both shook hands heartily. "It seems great to see you again."

"I can say the same thing about you," replied Frank Brandon. "You're tanned like a life guard at Coney Island. I'll bet you haven't been far from salt water all summer."

"You're right there," smiled Bob. "I was in the water so much that it's a wonder I didn't turn into a fish. The whole bunch of us had a wonderful time of it."

"Good enough!" Brandon exclaimed, heartily. "Where's all the rest of your crowd this evening?"

"They'll be around soon now. I'm expecting them any minute. There's Joe's whistle now! I thought he'd be along soon."

As he finished speaking Joe came bounding up the porch two steps at a time, and he had hardly got inside and shaken hands with Brandon when Jimmy and Herb appeared together. There was great excitement while they exchanged greetings, and then they went into the parlor and were made welcome by Mr. and Mrs. Layton.

"It seems good to get back in this town again," said Brandon, in a voice that carried conviction. "You folks have made me so welcome ever since we became acquainted that it seems almost like my own home town."

"That's the way we want everybody to feel," smiled Mr. Layton. "Clintonia is a neighborly town, and we always do our best to make visitors feel at home."

"I hear you've done a good deal of traveling since you were here last," said Mrs. Layton.

"Yes, I had a little commission to execute for the government down in Miami," said Brandon. "A radio inspector is apt to be sent anywhere on short notice, you know."

"How is your cousin, Mr. Harvey, getting along?" asked Bob. "Has he got entirely over his experience of last summer, when Dan Cassey knocked him out and stole his money?"

"Oh, yes, he's all right now," responded Brandon. "I saw him only day before yesterday, and he couldn't get through talking about the way you fellows took charge of the station while he was down and out, and then got the money back afterward. That was mighty fine work, and you can believe both he and I are grateful to you for what you did."

"Oh, that wasn't much," disclaimed Bob. "Besides, he'd done so much for us that we owed him something in return."

"He didn't say anything about that," observed Brandon.

"I suppose that's the last thing in the world he would mention," laughed Joe. "But he gave us all kinds of stuff on radio, and even loaned us a practice set to get the code with."

"Don't forget about the motor boat," said Herb. "He was as generous with that as with everything else. We sure had some fine cruises in the old Sea Bird."

"That sounds like him, all right," admitted Brandon. "There's hardly anything you could ask him for that he wouldn't cheerfully give you. He told me that you fellows were getting to be regular sharps at the radio game. Are you building any sets at present?"

"You bet we are!" cried Bob. "Come on down to my workroom, and we'll show you what we're doing. We're working on a regular set this time."

"I'm with you," said Brandon, heartily. "Come ahead and let's see what you've got. I suppose you'll be giving me pointers pretty soon."

"Not for a little time yet, anyway," grinned Bob. "The government hasn't been after us yet begging us to take jobs in the radio department."

"You never can tell," replied Brandon. "There's a big demand for radio men these days, and we're getting some pretty young chaps in our division."

"We don't feel as though we'd much more than scratched the surface of radiophony yet," said Joe. "There's such an immense amount to be learned, and then there are new discoveries being made every day. It would take almost all a fellow's time just to keep up with new developments, let alone learn all the fundamentals."

"That will all come in time," said the radio inspector. "You're on the right road now, anyway, and traveling pretty fast. Say!" he exclaimed, a moment later, as he was ushered into the workroom and caught sight of the new set, which was partially completed. "You're certainly going into it pretty heavily this time, aren't you? I didn't imagine you were working up anything so elaborate."

"We thought we might as well make something pretty good while we were about it," said Bob. "It won't be much more work to make this set than a smaller one, and we expect to get a whole lot better results. Don't you think so yourself?"

"There's no doubt about it," agreed Mr. Brandon. "When you get this set finished, you ought to be able to catch pretty near anything that happens to be flying around. Let's see how you intend to hook things up."

The boys explained their ideas and methods in detail, while the radio man nodded appreciatively from time to time. Sometimes he interrupted to ask a question or make a suggestion, which was duly taken note of by the enthusiastic boys.

"There doesn't seem to be a whole lot that I can tell you," remarked Frank Brandon, after they had gone over everything in detail. "You seem to have thought it out very thoroughly already, and outside of the few minor things I've already told you, I can't think of much to suggest. It looks to me as though you'd have a pretty good set there when you get through.

"There's one tip I want to give you though," he went on. "And that is to be careful about your tuning. You've noticed, no doubt, that sometimes you get first-class results, and then again the reception is so unsatisfactory that you are disgusted. Now in nine times out of ten the whole trouble is that you haven't tuned your receiver properly. You can't do the thing in a haphazard fashion and get the signals clearly. You know what Michelangelo said about 'trifles that make perfection.' Well, it's something like that in tuning your receiver.

"Now I see that in this receiver you have separate controls for the primary and secondary circuits. To tune in correctly you have to adjust both circuits to the wave length of the special signal that you are trying to get.

"First you start in with a tentative adjustment of the first primary. Fix it, let us say, for between a third and a half of its maximum value. I see that here the coupling between the primary and secondary is adjustable, so place it at maximum at the start. Of course you know that maximum means the position in which the windings are closest to each other.

"Then you fix up the secondary circuit for adjustment to the wave length, turning it slowly from minimum to maximum until you come to the point where the desired station is heard. When this is found, you again readjust the primary until you find the point of maximum loudness.

"Now you see the advantage of this double control. If an interfering station butts in, just decrease the coupling between primary and secondary and then tune again the two circuits. You can feel pretty sure of cutting out the interference and getting clearly just the station that you want."

"That's mighty good dope," said Bob. "I've had that trouble more than once and haven't been quite clear as to the best way of getting around it."

"Then too," went on the radio expert, "you must be careful in adjusting the tickler that gives the regenerative effect. Start in slowly by turning the control knob toward the maximum. You'll soon strike a point where the signal will be loud and clear. Now when you've got to that point, don't overdo it. If you get too much regeneration, the quality of the notes becomes distorted and before you know it you have only a jumble. Let well enough alone is a good rule in tuning, as in many other things. When your coffee's sweet enough, another spoonful of sugar will only spoil it. Keep to the middle of the road. It isn't the loudest noise you want but the sweetest music.

"Be careful, too," he urged, "not to have too brilliant a filament. It's wholly unnecessary to have it at a white heat, and you don't want to burn it out any more quickly than you have to. You can save money in reducing the filament brightness by increasing the regeneration, which will make up for the loss of brilliancy.

"Now by keeping these things in mind," he concluded, "you'll be able to operate your set to the best advantage and get the satisfaction you are looking for."

"We certainly hope to, anyway," said Bob. "We've put a lot of work and quite a little money into this outfit, and we'd be mightily disappointed if we didn't get good results."

"There's not much doubt about that, I think," remarked Frank Brandon. "You ought to see some of the sets I come across! They look to be regular nightmares, but they get passable results, anyway. Radio is certainly getting to be a country-wide craze. Only the other day I was at one of the big broadcasting stations, and the manager told me that they were actually having trouble to get performers, there is such a demand for them. They seem to be especially hard up for novelty acts—something out of the ordinary. People get tired of the same old programmes night after night."

"Say!" exclaimed Bob, struck by a sudden thought. "Why wouldn't that be just the thing for Larry when he gets a little better? He could do his bird imitations just as well as ever, and he could do it as well sitting in a chair, as far as that goes."

"Bob, you said something!" exclaimed Joe, slapping him on the back. "That's just the kind of thing that would appeal to people, too. I'll bet he'd be a hit from the beginning."

"Who is Larry?" asked Mr. Brandon, curiously.

The excited boys told him all about their acquaintance with Larry and Tim up to the time of the almost fatal accident in the theater. Brandon listened attentively, and when they had finished sat thinking for several minutes.

"Yes, I think it could be arranged all right," he said at last. "I know the manager of one big New Jersey broadcasting station personally, and I'm sure he'd be willing to give your friend a try-out. If he's as good as you say he is, they'd probably be glad to put him on the pay roll. From what you tell me, his act is certainly a novelty, and that's what they want."

CHAPTER XII

A GLAD ANNOUNCEMENT

"We'll go and see Larry as soon as we get out of school to-morrow, and see what he says about it," said Bob. "But I guess there's no doubt of what he'll want to do. I know he's mighty worried about the future. He told me he didn't have much money saved up, and what he did have must be about gone by this time."

"You do that," agreed Brandon. "And if he thinks favorably of the idea, I'll find time to go with him and you to the station I spoke of, and give him an introduction to the manager and see that he gets a try-out."

"That's mighty good of you, Mr. Brandon," said Joe. "Larry is such a fine fellow that when you get to know him you'll feel as interested in seeing him get along as we are."

"That's likely enough," said Brandon. "Anyway, if we didn't help each other out a little, this old world wouldn't be much of a place to live in."

After a little further conversation, Brandon rose to go. "I've got a pretty busy day ahead of me to-morrow, so I think I'd better turn in rather early to-night," he said. "Just give me a call at the hotel any time you want me, or, better yet, come and pay me a visit in person. You know you'll always be welcome."

"You bet we'll come," promised Jimmy.

"Jimmy's thinking of some special milk chocolate you gave him once, and is hoping you may have some more of it," laughed Joe.

"I wasn't thinking anything of the kind!" exclaimed Jimmy, indignantly. "What do you think I am, anyway?"

"We'd hate to tell you that," said Herb, with a wicked grin. "It would hurt your feelings too much, Doughnuts."

"I think I know what chocolate he refers to," said Brandon, laughing. "And I don't wonder that you remember it, Jimmy. It certainly was good, but I'm afraid you won't be able to find any more like it around here. It was sent to me from Vermont by a married sister of mine who lives there."

"Poor old Jimmy!" exclaimed Bob. "You're out of luck this time, old timer. If you had only known that, you wouldn't have had to make that heartbreaking search all over Clintonia."

"Oh, I didn't mind it so much," said his good-natured friend. "I had a lot of fun sampling all the different varieties, anyway."

"I'll say you did," said Herb. "I'll bet you were glad of an excuse."

"Don't need an excuse," retorted Jimmy. "I guess there's no law against eating chocolate, is there?"

"If there were, you'd be serving a life sentence now," said Joe, heartlessly.

"From the way you talk, I guess you don't like chocolate, so you won't want any of this," and Jimmy proceeded to unwrap a sizable bundle that he had brought with him, but had forgotten in the excitement of Brandon's visit.

"I didn't say that, did I?" asked Joe, in a tone of injured innocence.

"No such luck," said Jimmy. "Maybe if you didn't want any, the rest of us might get enough for once. But I suppose you'll want it all, as usual."

"Nothing of the kind," denied Joe. "I'm perfectly willing to go on a fifty-fifty basis. Half for me and half for the rest is all I ask. That's perfectly fair, isn't it?"

"It's fair enough for you, perhaps, but it doesn't make much of a hit with us," laughed Bob. "Don't take any notice of him, Jimmy. Just take your knife and break that chocolate up into lumps, and let's find out what it tastes like."

"You'd better wait a few minutes and sample this, Mr. Brandon," said Jimmy, doing as Bob directed. "I'll guarantee that it's the best to be gotten in Clintonia, anyway. I've shopped around this town looking for your brand of chocolate until I'm an expert in that line."

The chocolate disappeared as if by magic, and Frank Brandon rose once more to go.

"I'm really going this time," he laughed. "It won't make any difference if you bring out a dozen packages, Jimmy."

"I only wish I had 'em to bring out," sighed that individual.

"I wish you had, too," said Herb. "Why didn't you get some more while you were about it, Doughnuts?"

"You fellows are certainly hard to please," laughed Brandon. "But I must go now. I hope you'll all drop into the hotel when you get a chance, and we'll smooth out some more radio kinks. I have some good books in my trunk, too, that might be of some help."

"We'll be glad to come," said Bob, heartily. "We'll all drop in some evening around the first of the week, shan't we, fellows?"

Of course, they all agreed to this, and then Brandon took his leave, accompanied by Joe and Herb and Jimmy as far as their respective homes.

The next day the radio boys were eager to tell Larry about the conversation they had had with Frank Brandon concerning him, and the bright prospects the radio man had held out for his successful employment. They could hardly wait for three o'clock to come, and the bell had hardly rung when they were all out in the street ready to make a quick trip to the hospital.

"Come on, fellows," called Bob. "They say that bad news travels fast, but let's prove that good news can hit it up once in a while, too. I'll bet old Larry will be happier this evening than he has been for a long time."

"That speed stuff is all right for you fellows, but don't forget that I'm built more for comfort than speed," grumbled Jimmy. "Set your own pace, though, Bob, and I'll try to keep up, even if it kills me."

"It will be more apt to do you good," said Herb, as they all set off at a brisk dog trot. "There's no doubt that you need more exercise than you get, Doughnuts."

"I get more than I want already," said Jimmy, who was beginning to puff and pant. The others had no mercy on him, though, and when at last they reached the hospital poor Doughnuts was, as he himself said, "all in."

Larry was glad to see them. He was feeling rather blue for, in a roundabout way, a report had reached him that Buck Looker was still connecting himself and Tim with the loss of the watch and other things of value at the hotel dance. Buck had intimated that the two vaudeville performers might have passed the stolen things over to some confederate.

"It's certainly wonderful to have you fellows spend so much of your time with a poor old cripple like me," he said, with a smile in which there was a trace of tears. "I don't know what I'd ever do if you didn't. Tim's a good sort about writing, but I am lonesome and every hour seems to me like a day."

"What do you mean, 'old cripple'?" scoffed Bob. "Why, the doctor says he'll have you out of here and as good as ever in a little while."

"A 'little while' may mean almost anything," said Larry, with a sad smile. "But I'm not kicking, you understand," he added, quickly. "I know I'm mighty lucky to be alive."

"You're not only alive, but you're going to be mighty busy pretty soon, if you happen to feel like holding down a good job," said Bob.

CHAPTER XIII

FULL OF PROMISE

"What do you mean 'good job'?" asked Larry, incredulously, and yet with a note of hope in his voice. "You know I can't even get around easily yet."

"Yes, but you're getting stronger every day," argued Bob. "In a week or so you won't know yourself. Now, here's the proposition we've got for you," and Bob proceeded to outline the plan that they had worked out the previous evening. As he proceeded, a light came into the sick boy's eyes that had not been there since the accident, and a touch of color crept into his cheeks.

"Say!" he broke out, when Bob had finished, "you fellows are about the best friends that anybody ever had."

"Oh, nonsense!" exclaimed Bob. "Why, you know well enough that you'd do anything in the world for one of us if our positions were reversed."

"Well, it will be simply wonderful for me," said Larry. "Of course, though, I may be counting the chickens before they are hatched. The manager of the station may not like my act, you know."

"It's more a question of whether the public will like it or not," said Joe. "Mr. Brandon seems to be sure that the manager will give you a try-out, and I guess they'll soon find out whether your act is popular or not. Judging from the applause you got in the theater that night, I should certainly say it was."

"I only wish I were strong enough to go right away," said Larry. "But I guess I won't be able to go this week, anyway."

"We didn't suppose you would," said Bob. "But Mr. Brandon is going to make his headquarters in Clintonia for several weeks, so you don't have to worry about that. As soon as the doctor says you can make the trip, we'll see if we can't borrow or beg an automobile somewhere, and make the trip to the sending station in style."

"Now that I've got something to look forward to, I'll get well in a hurry," Larry assured him.

"Let's see if you can still make the little birdies jealous by singing their songs better than they can," suggested Jimmy.

"You certainly flatter me, but I'll do the best I can," laughed Larry. "What shall it be first?"

"How about the mocking bird?" suggested Herb. "I think that's one of the prettiest ones, Larry. I never heard a southern mocking bird, but if it sounds like that, I'm going to take a trip to Dixieland some day just to hear one."

"I never heard one, either," confessed Larry, with a grin.

"You didn't!" they all exclaimed. "Where did you learn it, then?"

"A professional bird imitator taught me most of the notes," said Larry. "Of course, I didn't need any lessons to imitate the cute little canary bird, and the robin's notes and a few others I learned by listening to the birds themselves. I suppose it would be best to learn them all that way, if you could, but I never had the time or the money to go traveling all over the country."

"Well, we're still waiting for the mocking bird," Herb reminded him. "I'll sing 'Listen to the Mocking Bird,' and you come in at the proper places with the bird effects."

"Nobody asked you to sing, did they?" asked Jimmy.

"No, they didn't; but I'm going to sing, anyway," answered Herb, and he started the first bars of the well known song.

"We might as well all sing, then," said Bob. "We can't make it any worse than Herb's singing, anyway," so they all joined in the song. At the end of each line they paused, and Larry gave the proper bird notes and trills. The result was not half bad, and before they had finished other convalescent patients had come into the room and were listening appreciatively. The boys all had their backs to the door, and did not know they had an audience until they came to the end of the song and there was a round of applause for their effort.

They all whirled around in some surprise.

"I didn't know we were making anybody suffer but ourselves," laughed Bob. "It must be pretty hard on you folks."

"It sounded fine," said one. "We enjoyed it. Why don't you try something else?"

"Couldn't think of it," said Bob. "Besides, I guess that's about the only song we all know except the 'Star Spangled Banner,' and there aren't any bird songs in that. You give them some more imitations, though, Larry. You will be all the better for the practice, anyway."

"Anything to oblige," grinned Larry, and went through his whole repertoire, while the little audience applauded freely.

"There! that's all I know," said Larry at last, when he had imitated every kind of bird he could think of. "I'll have to get busy and learn some more, I guess."

"We didn't know we had such a talented young man in the place," said one elderly gentleman. "You'll have to entertain us every day while you're here, young man."

"Well, if you folks can stand it, I can," laughed Larry. "I'll always be glad to oblige, I'm sure."

His appreciative listeners thanked him, and gradually drifted out of the room.

"You made a hit, Larry," said Bob. "It's just as I tell you. Your art is a novelty, and people are tickled to death with it. You won't have to worry about making good when you get your try-out at the broadcasting station."

"I hope you're right," said Larry. "I can't wait until I'm strong enough, to take the trip. Anyway, I'll have something to look forward to now."

The time had passed so quickly that the boys could hardly believe it when Bob looked at his watch and told them it was nearly six o'clock.

"Good-night!" exclaimed Joe. "We'll all be late for supper now. Guess we'll have to say good-bye and beat it, Larry."

"I suppose so," said Larry, regretfully. "I want to thank you all again for what you've done for me, and believe me, I appreciate it."

They all shook hands with him, and then started for home at a brisk pace.

"Seems to me we're always in a hurry," complained Jimmy. "You pretty near run my legs off getting here, and now I've got to repeat the performance going home, or else get a cold supper when I get there. I wonder why I'm always out of luck that way."

"You'd better save your breath, instead of wasting it in kicking," Joe admonished him. "You'll need it all before you get home, I'll tell you. Let's hit it up a little faster, fellows. Jimmy wants to get home before his supper gets cold, so we'll have to see that he gets there."

"Come on, Doughnuts, step on the throttle," cried Herb. "Show us what you really can do."

"Nothing doing," panted Jimmy. "My throttle's wide open now. You fellows go ahead if you're in such a hurry."

"I guess there's no such rush as that," said Bob, slowing down to a pace more suited to Jimmy's limited speed. "Take it easy, old man. We're not going to a fire, after all."

CHAPTER XIV

AN IMPROMPTU FEAST

"Anybody would think we were, to look at us," puffed Jimmy. "Whew, I'm all in!" and he slowed down to a walk.

"Well, we're almost home, anyway," said Bob. "Take your time, Jimmy. We'd hate to have you die of apoplexy."

"You wouldn't hate it nearly as much as I would," said Jimmy, beginning to get his breath again. "Just think of what the world would lose if anything were to happen to me."

"It's too terrible to think about," said Bob, with mock gravity. "I suppose the old world would stop spinning if you should kick the bucket, Jimmy."

"Maybe not as bad as that," interposed Herb. "But a lot of doughnut manufacturers would have to go out of business, I know that."

"Aw, you know too much!" exclaimed Jimmy, scornfully. "At least, you think you do, which is worse. I don't see what you have to go to high school for, anyway. You know all there is to know, already."

"I don't know but what you're right," agreed Herb, complacently. "But the trouble is, I can't seem to get the teachers to believe it. Maybe you'll be nice enough to explain things to them to-morrow, Jimmy?"

"Explain nothing!" exclaimed Jimmy. "They'd soon think I was as foolish as you, and I'd hate to get a rep. like that."

"Harsh words," laughed Bob. "You fellows had better quit saying nice things about one another, or you'll be mixing it first thing you know."

"No chance," denied Herbert, with a grin. "I'm too hungry to think of scrapping, and I'll bet Jimmy is too. How about it, old pal?"

"I should say so!" agreed Jimmy. "Thank heaven we're almost home. If we had much further to go, I guess you'd have to carry me."

They were indeed almost home by this time, and branched off to their respective houses. Though they were all late, they managed to make up for lost time in the way of eating and their mothers had reason to be thankful that they were not late very often.

An interesting bit of information came about this time in the news conveyed by Mr. Rockwell to Mr. Layton, whom he had chanced to meet on a train, that the motor boat which had run down Larry and his companions had been found in a remote inlet some distance down the coast, where it had evidently been deserted by the men who had stolen it. From sundry papers that had been left on the boat, through an oversight of the rascals, it was gathered that they were members of a gang of hotel thieves who had been "working" the hotels at the summer resorts along the coast, where a long list of unsolved robberies had been perpetrated. The police were working on the case, but the thieves had not yet been apprehended.

"Well," said Bob, when he heard the news, "it's good to know that Mr. Wentworth got his motor boat back anyway. But I won't be satisfied till I hear that the police have landed the thieves."

"Same here," said Joe. "But it's like looking for a needle in a haystack. They may be out on the Pacific coast by this time."

The boys worked hard on their big set for the next few days, spending all the time on it that they could spare from their studies. They found time, however, to visit Mr. Brandon, as they had promised, and had a royal good time in his rooms at the hotel. They laughed and joked and talked radio to their hearts' content. Toward the end of the evening Mr. Brandon called on Jimmy for some expert advice.

"Jimmy," he said, "I've been thinking that a little—or rather, a lot—of ice cream and cake would go well. What is your honest opinion on the subject?"

"I don't think you could have a much better idea, no matter how hard you tried," said Jimmy, gravely.

"Probably not," agreed Brandon, with a twinkle in his eyes. "Now, as we're agreed as to that, can I call on you for advice and assistance?"

"You certainly can," said Jimmy, slightly mystified, but ready for anything, nevertheless.

"Well, then, to come to the point, will you go out with me and give me the benefit of your expert advice as to the best place in this neighborhood to buy the aforementioned ice cream and cake?"

"You bet I will," said Jimmy, with alacrity. "And without seeming to boast," he added, "you couldn't have picked out any one who knows more about that particular subject than yours truly."

"All right, I suppose I'll have to believe you," laughed Frank Brandon. "I have every confidence in you, Jimmy."

As the event proved, this confidence was not misplaced. Both the ice cream and cake were all that heart could wish, and moreover were served in generous quantities. At the end of the feast they all expressed themselves as perfectly satisfied with Jimmy's selections, and Bob moved that they give him and Mr. Brandon a vote of thanks.

"If Uncle Sam lets me stay in Clintonia long enough, we'll have to have another party like this," said Brandon. "And maybe by that time your sick friend will be well enough to come. I'd surely be glad to see him, if he can and would care to. By the way, when will he be well enough for us to take him to the broadcasting station?"

"We were out to see him yesterday," answered Bob; "and it's wonderful the improvement he's made since we told him about our plans for him. He looked a hundred per cent. better, and the doctor told him he could go Saturday afternoon, if he kept on making the same progress."

"Fine!" exclaimed the wireless man. "I usually have Saturday afternoons off, and if you boys want to take him then, it will be all right for me, unless something very important comes up that I can't sidetrack."

"That suits us," said Bob. "I spoke to Doctor Dale about Larry the other day, and he volunteered to drive us to the station in his car. That was some offer, wasn't it?"

"It's no more than I'd expect of him," said Brandon. "Right after we first talked about that plan I wrote to the manager of the station, Mr. Allard, and he said to bring your friend along by all means. He's on the lookout for talent, as I told you, and will be only too glad to give him a trial."

"That sounds promising," said Bob. "What do you say if we stop at the hospital to-morrow afternoon, fellows, and tell Larry about it and find out if he'll be strong enough to go?"

"I'm afraid you'll have to count me out," said Jimmy. "I've got some work I'll have to do for dad, if we're going to be away Saturday afternoon. But you fellows go anyway, and tell him I was sorry that I couldn't get there."

"We'll do that then, and count on you sure for Saturday afternoon," said Bob.

"Oh, sure thing! I'll be with you then," promised Jimmy. "I wouldn't miss that for a farm."

That matter being satisfactorily settled, the boys said good-night to their host, after assuring him that they had had a "bang-up" time. Their leave-taking must have wakened any light sleepers in the hotel, but they got out at last and headed for home, all of them enthusiastic in praise of their friend Frank Brandon.

"I only wish we could have had Larry here to-night," said Joe, regretfully. "I'll bet he'd have enjoyed it first rate. But I suppose there'll be plenty of other times."

"I wish Mr. Brandon were going to be stationed in Clintonia all the time," said Bob. "He's been such a good friend to us that I'll feel mighty bad if he has to go away again."

They all felt the same way, and said so.

"But there's no use crossing that bridge until we come to it," said Joe, philosophically. "As long as he's covering this territory, he'll make his headquarters in Clintonia, that's pretty certain."

The next day the boys met as they had planned, immediately after school was out, and headed directly for the hospital and their convalescent friend. What with jokes and laughter the distance seemed short enough. Needless to say, Larry was overjoyed to see them.

"I certainly look forward to having you fellows visit me," he said. "You're as welcome as letters from home. I get pretty blue sitting around here by my lonesome all day."

"How do you feel to-day?" asked Bob. "Do you feel well enough to go after a soft job next Saturday?"

"I never did feel so sick that I couldn't go after a job that was guaranteed to be soft," grinned Larry.

"All right, then," laughed Bob. "Be ready to go next Saturday afternoon. We'll call for you in Doctor Dale's automobile. He's promised to take the whole bunch of us to the broadcasting station."

"Pretty soft," said Larry. "How do you fellows come to rate an automobile?"

"Oh, we've got a big drag around this town," replied Bob. "I guess they'd give us the Town Hall if we asked for it."

"You hate yourselves, don't you?" asked Larry.

"That isn't as big a claim as it may seem," remarked Joe. "The Town Hall is so old that I think they'd be glad of an excuse to give it away. But they won't build a new one until the old one falls down."

"That's the way with all these bush league towns," remarked Larry, with a wicked grin.

"You're getting well all right," laughed Bob. "When you begin knocking again it's a sure sign that you're getting back to form."

"You bet I am," returned Larry. "I'll be as good as ever in a little while. Now that I can begin to see where the next square meal is coming from, it gives me some incentive to get well."

"Well, it's fine to hear you say so," declared Bob. "We'll call for you around one o'clock Saturday, and we'll be at the station about four. Then if you don't convince them that your imitation of bird songs is better than the little birdies themselves, we'll murder you."

"I wish I could get in as solid with every audience I play to as I am with you fellows," said Larry. "Life would be one grand, sweet song."

"You'll get in solid enough to be able to drag down good pay, don't worry about that," replied Joe.

"Well, we'll know more about it after Saturday afternoon," said Larry. "Until then, hope hard."

This seemed to sum up the situation fairly well, and after a little further conversation the radio boys said good-by to their friend and took their leave, delighted over his improved condition.

Improved not only in body but in mind. The pain of his physical hurts had been hard enough for Larry to bear, but this was little compared to the mental worry he had been undergoing ever since the accident had interfered with his money-earning power and threatened to make him a cripple for life.

During his brief engagement with the Chasson show he had loyally sent home to his mother every dollar he could save from his salary over and above his necessary expenses, which by rigid economy he kept as low as possible. But much of this his mother had been compelled to use to pay debts incurred during his previous period of idleness, and he knew that she had very little on hand. Her enfeebled condition had added to his anxiety, and he had had many hours of mental anguish as he looked toward the dark and lowering future.

Now, however, he saw light, and his heart went out in the warmest gratitude toward the good friends who had come to his help in his extremity and made it possible to see a rainbow in the skies that had been so full of clouds.

"Now, if I could only prove that Tim and I weren't guilty of that robbery at the hotel dance, I would be all right," Larry told himself. He felt sure that the evil-minded Buck Looker was still holding that happening against him.

The days intervening until Saturday sped quickly. Dr. Dale was true to the promise he had made Bob, and was ready with his car when the radio boys assembled at his house. Since Bob had told him about Larry's unfortunate condition, the doctor had interested himself in the case and had been to visit Larry once or twice at the hospital. He had conceived a liking for the injured boy, which had made him accede all the more readily to Bob's request for the automobile.

CHAPTER XV

GETTING A TRIAL

Doctor Dale met the boys at the door as they came up.

"I'll be ready in a few minutes," he told them, as he admitted them to the parlor. "Make yourselves comfortable while I get my hat and coat on, and we'll get started."

He left the room, only to reappear a few moments later in full motoring regalia.

"All ready," he announced. "Come on out to the garage and we'll get started. Mr. Brandon called me up this morning, and he'll be waiting for us at his hotel."

The boys piled into the big seven passenger touring car and were whisked down to Mr. Brandon's hotel. He was ready and waiting and jumped into the car almost before it had stopped. From there they sped quickly to the hospital, and Bob and Joe helped Larry into the car.

"This is certainly a wonderful day for me," said Larry. "I don't know how I'll ever be able to thank you folks for all that you have done for me."

"Don't even try to," said Bob. "Don't worry about it, and we'll agree not to."

"Well, we'll let it go at that," said Larry. "But if I don't say any more, you'll know I'm grateful, anyway."

"You've got nothing to be grateful about yet," Joe reminded him. "They may throw you out, and that's nothing to be thankful for."

"Ouch!" exclaimed Larry. "Please don't mention it."

"Don't cross that bridge till we come to it," advised Jimmy. "I've got some chocolate almond bars that I'll guarantee will make you forget all your troubles while you're eating them."

"That's Jimmy's remedy for all troubles," said Herb. "Eat and forget them is his motto."

"Well, it isn't such a bad one," remarked Frank Brandon. "I've often known my troubles to look a lot less serious after a square meal."

"You bet," agreed Jimmy. "I know I *always* feel better myself after a square meal."

"I guess we all do," said Dr. Dale. "And that reminds me that I want you all to come to my house for supper to-night after we get back."

"I guess we'll be glad to go all right," said the radio expert. "But when you see what we do to the food, you'll probably be sorry you asked us."

"I'll take a chance on that," laughed Dr. Dale. "I generally have a pretty good appetite myself after a motoring trip, and you young fellows will have to step some to beat me."

"Well, we'll back Jimmy against any entry," grinned Bob. "We plan to enter him in a pie-eating contest some day, and when we do we'll bet a lot of money on him to win."

"I'll do my best to justify your confidence," retorted Jimmy. "I wouldn't mind backing myself with a small piece of change. Pies just seem to be my natural prey."

"Wait till I get well again," said Larry. "And you'll have some competition from me. It has always been my highest ambition to be around some day when a pie wagon gets hit by an automobile."

"Jerusalem!" said Jimmy. "That would be heaven on earth, wouldn't it?"

"That's probably your idea of it," said Joe. "I suppose you'd rather have streets paved with pie than with gold."

"Oh, well, what's the use of talking about it?" sighed Jimmy. "It's all too good to be true anyway."

"It's a wonder you fellows wouldn't cut out that talk and look at the landscape a little," said Bob. "You're missing some pretty fine scenery."

"It is beautiful," remarked Frank Brandon. "It's too bad we haven't got further to go, as long as Doctor Dale is buying the gasoline."

"Oh, it's cheap at any price," laughed Dr. Dale. "I don't know what I would ever do without this car."

The miles rolled rapidly behind them, and before they realized it they were on the outskirts of New York. The boys thoroughly enjoyed the ride through the city; probably more than did Dr. Dale, to whom the heavy traffic was anything but a pleasure. They finally reached the downtown ferries, however, and after a slight wait in line, got on a boat. The boys were absorbed by the busy scene presented by the river which was covered with craft of all descriptions. The big ferryboat edged its way across the river without mishap and bumped into its slip. The traffic on the New Jersey side was hardly less dense than that which they had encountered in New York, but Dr. Dale skillfully threaded his way through it and after a drive through narrow streets lined by foundries and factories, and across the broad meadows, and past more places of business, they at last drew up before the big broadcasting station.

"Well, here we are," said Dr. Dale, relaxing after the strain of traffic driving. "How do you feel, Larry? Strong for anything?"

"I'm a little shaky, but I guess I'll get through with it all right," replied Larry. "Just lead me to it."

The boys assisted him into the radio station, where Mr. Brandon introduced them all to the manager, Mr. Allard.

"You're just in time," said the latter. "We need somebody to substitute in our program to-night, as one of the regular performers is ill. Come up to the sending room and we'll give your young friend a trial."

"Go to it, old boy," encouraged Bob, in a whisper. "Show him what's what. Remember that we're all rooting for you."

Larry pressed his hand, but had no time to answer before they were ushered up to the sending room. One wall of this apartment was covered with complicated-looking electrical apparatus, a good deal of which the boys recognized but which appeared very mysterious to poor Larry.

"For testing purposes, our apparatus is so rigged up that we can hear, in this room, exactly what goes out over the wires," the manager explained. "If you gentlemen will sit at that table over there, and all put on headphones, you can hear your friend's performance exactly as it will sound to everybody else who is listening to this station."

"Did you get that?" whispered the irrepressible Herb. "He called us gentlemen."

"Shut up," whispered Bob. "He didn't mean you, anyway."

Following the manager's instructions, Larry took up his position at a short distance from an instrument called a microphone, and at a signal from Mr. Allard commenced his bird imitations.

The manager had donned earphones like all the rest, and the little company listened with varying emotions as Larry went through his repertoire. His friends were praying fervently for his success and were delighted as they realized that he was surpassing any of his previous efforts. The manager's attitude was critical, but as Larry went from one imitation to another the boys could see from the expression of his face that he was pleased. Larry rose to his opportunity nobly, and as he realized that he was making a good impression added trills and notes that he had never thought of before. By the time he had finished, all doubt had vanished from Mr. Allard's mind.

"I guess we can use you all right, young man," he said. "Do you think you can fill in this evening? I need somebody to round out the bedtime programme at seven o'clock, and I imagine your act ought to go well at that time."

"Anything you say, sir," answered Larry, "will suit me."

"I can put you up here for to-night," volunteered Mr. Allard. "And if you don't feel strong enough to work regularly for a week or so, you can go back to-morrow and report for your regular performance a week from to-day."

"I think that would be best," put in Frank Brandon. "I imagine Mr. Bartlett will need at least another week before he'll be able to work steadily."

Larry was but little older than the radio boys, and Herb was in an ecstasy of delight over Brandon's "Mr. Bartlett."

"But if you stay here to-night you'll miss having dinner at Doctor Dale's house!" cried Jimmy, impulsively.

"Guess it can't be helped," said Larry, with a laugh, in which the others joined. "Business before pleasure, you know, Jimmy."

"That's what dad always tells me, too," grumbled Jimmy. "But personally, I'd rather have the pleasure first, and let the business take its chance afterward."

"Don't you believe it," said Mr. Allard. "There are too many people doing that already. It's a system that will never help you to put money in the bank, my boy."

"He'll probably find that out for himself sooner or later," said Mr. Brandon. "I used to feel the same way, but I've got over it."

"We'll all be sorry that you can't be with us to-night, Larry," said Dr. Dale, kindly. "But we'll be home in time to listen to your first radio performance this evening, so you'll know that we're hearing you just the same as though we were in this room with you."

"I'll be sure of that, Doctor Dale," said Larry. "But I know I'll be missing a fine supper at your house, and you know how I'd like to be there. I'll be back in Clintonia to-morrow, anyway."

"But how are you going to travel back alone?" asked Bob. "You're not strong enough to go sailing around all by your lonesome yet."

"Don't let that worry you," replied Mr. Allard. "I'll see that somebody goes to the train with him, and I guess one of you fellows won't mind meeting him at the train at the other end."

"I rather guess not," said Bob, emphatically. "We'll be there with bells on, Larry; you can bet on that."

"It seems as though I'm making you all a lot of trouble," said Larry. "I guess I could get along all right."

"We'll be there, so there's no use of your saying any more about it," said Bob, in a voice of finality. "How about it, fellows?"

All the radio boys were of the same mind, so Larry was forced to give in.

"But if you're going to get back to Clintonia in time to hear my act at seven o'clock, you'll have to leave pretty soon," he said. "I'm not going to detain you here any longer."

"I'm afraid we will have to be going," said Dr. Dale, glancing at his watch. "The ferries are apt to be crowded at this hour, too. But we'll wish you all success at your new venture, Larry. If you always do as well as you did this afternoon, you'll soon be acquiring a big reputation."

They all shook hands with Larry and Mr. Allard, and went out to where Dr. Dale's automobile was waiting for them.

"I guess Larry was right when he said we'd have to make time going back," said Mr. Brandon. "It's three o'clock now, which doesn't leave us much of a margin."

"That's very true," conceded Dr. Dale. "But if we can have any luck in getting over the ferry and through New York traffic, we'll make it. Once out of the city, and I'll show you what my car can do in the way of eating up miles."

CHAPTER XVI

SPEED

Fortunately they met with very little delay in crossing the ferry, and Dr. Dale, in going through New York, avoided as far as possible the more congested thoroughfares. In a comparatively short time they had reached the outskirts, and Dr. Dale began to speed up a bit. As they reached the more open country, Dr. Dale opened the throttle wider, and the big car responded with a dash and power that delighted the boys. Mile after mile they reeled off, the wind whistling in their ears and making conversation difficult. The boys did not mind this, however, as they were enjoying the excitement of speed too much to have any desire to talk.

Slowing down for the towns, but speeding up again on the open road, the big car put mile after mile behind it, until the boys began to recognize the towns they passed through.

"Say!" yelled Joe, trying to make himself heard above the roar of the motor and the whistling of the wind, "aren't we making time, though? At this rate we'll get home with time to spare."

"You bet!" shouted Bob. "Isn't this a peach of a ride?"

"Only about six miles more to Clintonia," shouted Frank Brandon, from the front seat which he shared with Dr. Dale.

Most of that six miles consisted of new concrete state road as smooth and level as a billiard table. Up and up crept the speedometer needle, and the big car seemed to be fairly flying. Fences and trees flashed past them, and the smooth road seemed like a river flowing toward them. The boys were intoxicated with the wild thrill and exhilaration of speed, and laughed and shouted and pounded each other on the back. For several miles the speedometer needle never receded, and not until the roofs and church steeples of Clintonia were visible in the distance did Dr. Dale slacken pace and bring the big machine down to a sedate twenty-five miles an hour.

"Well, how did you like that?" he inquired, turning around for a moment to glance at the excited boys. "Was that fast enough to please you?"

"It was great!" declared Bob. "This car can certainly step along when you want it to."

"We'll be at my house in less than ten minutes. I hope you all feel as though you could eat a little something."

"Eat!" exclaimed Jimmy, in heartfelt tones. "Why, I'm so hungry I've been tempted to start in and eat the upholstery once or twice."

"Please don't," laughed Dr. Dale. "It's too expensive, besides being indigestible. Control yourself for a few minutes, and I'll promise you something much better than leather to eat."

"All right, then, I'll do the best I can," promised Jimmy, with a grin.

"We have to pass Antonio's shoe repairing store before we get to Doctor Dale's house, and if you like, I'll get out and buy you a nice big chunk of sole leather, Jimmy," suggested Joe. "If you really want something along that line, it seems a shame not to let you have it."

"Thanks all the same, but I wouldn't like to put you to all that trouble," said Jimmy, with elaborate politeness.

Joe was about to protest that he would not mind the trouble in the least, but before he had time to the car drew up in front of Dr. Dale's house.

Mrs. Dale was waiting for them on the front porch.

"I was beginning to get worried over you," she said. "But I suppose you found it quite a long trip, didn't you?"

"I can't say that it seemed very long to us," replied Mr. Brandon, smiling. "When you're in a car, you don't seem to think of the time much."

"Yes, I've noticed that myself," she admitted. "But you've arrived in time for supper, and that's the main thing. How did your young friend make out? Didn't you bring him back with you?"

"No, they intend to include him in the bedtime programme for kiddies this evening," explained Brandon. "It starts at seven o'clock, and Larry's performance should come in about half past seven. We'll just about have time to eat before we start listening for him."

In a very few minutes they were all seated about Dr. Dale's hospitable table, and it is hardly necessary to record the fact that they did full justice to their hostess' cooking. As they neared the end of the meal, Dr. Dale glanced at his watch.

"I know it is considered very impolite to hurry one's guests," he said; "but just the same, it is so near now to the time that Larry is scheduled that I propose that we postpone dessert until after we have heard him. Then we can take our time, and do both Larry and the dessert full justice."

They all acceded laughingly to this proposition, and a few minutes later filed into the room where the doctor kept his radio apparatus. His set was equipped with a loud talking device, so that individual headphones were not necessary.

With a few touches he adjusted his coils and condensers, and had no difficulty in picking up the broadcasting station. At the moment some one was telling a "bedtime story" for the little folks, and, as it happened, this was the last thing on the programme preceding Larry's act.

When the narrator had finished, there came a short pause, and then the familiar voice of the announcer.

"The next number on this programme will be a novelty, an imitation of various bird calls and songs, given by Mr. Larry Bartlett."

The sonorous voice of the announcer ceased, and the little group in Dr. Dale's house waited expectantly for the first notes of their friend's performance.

"Hooray!" shouted Jimmy, as the first notes of the mocking bird's song floated clear and true from the horn. "Hooray for Larry, the champion whistler of the universe!"

The others laughed at his enthusiasm, but they were almost as excited themselves. When at last their friend concluded his performance with a trill and a flourish, they all gave the three cheers that Jimmy had suggested, and wished they had a sending set so that they could congratulate Larry on the spot.

"That surely sounded well," said Dr. Dale, when their delight had somewhat subsided. "This may be the beginning of big things for Larry, because it will not take him long to become known when he has an audience of somewhere around a half a million people every evening."

"That's true enough," said Frank Brandon. "But it seems hard to realize that science has really made such a thing possible."

"I'm ready to believe that nothing is impossible these days," said Dr. Dale. "If I read in the paper some day that we had got into wireless communication with Mars, I should believe it easily enough. In fact, I'd hardly feel surprised."

"I'm sure I shouldn't," agreed the radio expert. "A person has to have a receptive mind to keep up with these quick-moving times."

"You're right," agreed Dr. Dale. "But now, as we've heard Larry and feel reasonably sure that his performance has been a success, I propose that we go back and have our dessert. Does that meet with your approval, Jimmy?"

"Does it!" exclaimed Jimmy. "I should say so. I never feel as though I'd really had anything much to eat unless I have dessert to top off with."

"After the dinner you ate, I don't really believe you could feel hungry, even if you didn't have dessert," said Herbert.

"That must be just one of your phony jokes," said Jimmy. "You know I was sitting beside you, Herb, and I felt pretty lucky to get anything to eat at all. Anybody within three places of you on each side doesn't have much of a show, you know."

"It's no use you're talking that way," said Herbert. "Everybody here knows you too well, Doughnuts. You've got a reputation as an eats hound that you'll never be able to live down."

"Oh, well, I don't care," said Jimmy, soothed by the sight of a big apple pie that was on the table. "That's better than having a reputation for making punk jokes like yours. If I eat too much, I'm the only one that gets a stomach ache from it, but your jokes give everybody a pain."

CHAPTER XVII

VAULTING AMBITION

"Bang!" exclaimed Bob, with a laugh. "That was saying something, Jimmy. You surely hit the bull's-eye plumb in the center that time. Guess that will hold you a while, Herb."

"It was a terrible slam," acknowledged Herb. "If I weren't so busy eating this pie, Jimmy, I'd be tempted to make you take back those cruel words."

"Nary take," said Jimmy, positively. "I said 'em, and I'll stick by 'em. Besides, it's so. Isn't it, Bob? I'll leave it to you."

"Well," said Bob, "in the interests of truth I'll have to admit that as a rule I'd rather have a stomach ache than listen to one of Herb's home-made jokes. But on the other hand, some of them aren't so awfully bad. If you took one and polished it up a bit here and there and changed it around a little, it might be good enough to raise a laugh in an insane asylum."

"It seems to me I remember once, a long time ago, when he made a joke that was so funny that we all laughed at it," said Joe. "It hardly seems possible, but I'm almost sure I remember it."

"Oh, you're all bugs, anyway, so that doesn't prove anything," said Herb, calmly finishing the last of his pie. "But some day, when I become a world-famous humorist, you'll realize how dumb you were not to appreciate my jokes. Now you get them free, but then it will cost you money to hear them."

"It will never cost me any money," said Bob, with conviction. "I wouldn't give a plugged nickel for a book full of them."

"Neither will anybody else," said Joe. "If you have any idea of ever making a living that way, Herb, you'd better forget it. You'd starve to death, sure."

"Well, it's a cinch I won't have to starve to death right now, anyway, so quit your croaking," retorted the much abused Herb. "Whoever told you fellows that you were judges of humor, anyway?"

"A person doesn't have to be an expert to judge your jokes," came back Joe. "If he knows anything at all, he can tell that they're rotten."

"All your friends seem to have very decided views on the question, Herbert," laughed Frank Brandon. "The popular vote seems to be heavily against you."

"Oh, their opinions aren't worth worrying about," said Herb, complacently. "As long as I know my jokes are good, I don't care what they say."

"That's the spirit," encouraged Brandon. "Remember, all great men have had to fight an uphill battle against criticism."

"That's true," said Herb, with a melancholy sigh. "And what's more, if you can judge by the amount of criticism, I must be going to be extra great. Still, that's likely enough, I suppose."

"Don't stop him, fellows," said Bob, with a mischievous grin. "Let him rave on. If he enjoys kidding himself that way, why should we wake him up?"

"Aw, you fellows who think you're so smart are probably kidding yourselves," said Herb. "Nobody could really be as smart as you Indians think you are and live to tell the story."

"That's one of the failings of human nature to rate ourselves too highly," interposed Dr. Dale, with a smile. "But now, how would you all like to go in and hear the rest of the concert? We've missed only the first part, and there's still quite a good deal to come."

They all acceded to this proposal with alacrity, and found that, as the doctor had said, they had not missed much of the programme. The wireless apparatus worked to perfection, and they could hear everything perfectly.

"The static isn't nearly as bad to-night as it was a month or two ago," said Dr. Dale. "At times last summer it interfered a good deal with my receiving."

"Yes, it's always a good deal worse in summer than in winter," remarked Frank Brandon. "I always advise beginners not to start at wireless in mid-summer, as they sometimes get such poor results with their small sets that they get discouraged and give up the game altogether. It's better to wait until fall, and then by the next summer they've had experience enough to know how to reduce the bad effects of static."

"It used to get pretty bad sometimes at Ocean Point last summer," observed Bob. "Once or twice our concerts were almost spoiled by it, while at other times we'd hardly notice it."

"With that set, you ought to be able to get any broadcasting station in the Eastern States," said Brandon. "And if you have luck, and conditions happened to be just right, you might even get something from the other side, although of course that isn't very likely."

"Oh, we've been talking about that, but we don't really expect to," said Joe. "We might be able to get the wireless telegraph signals from the other side, though, don't you think?"

"That's likely enough," answered Brandon. "The best time to get them is late at night, when the broadcasting and amateur stations are not sending. I've often sat and listened with Brandon Harvey to the big station at Nauen, Germany, or to the Eiffel Tower in Paris."

"Jimminy!" exclaimed Herb. "We'll have to bone down at our language courses at high school, fellows. I suppose that they send in whatever language the people speak where the sending station is located, don't they?"

"As a rule they do, but not always," replied Frank Brandon. "It depends to a great extent where the message is being sent to. If it is being sent to this country, it is often in English, while if it were being sent to France, it would be in French, naturally."

"Yes, I suppose it would have to be that way," said Bob, thoughtfully, "although I never thought about that side of it before. It won't make much difference what language they're sending in, though, so long as we know that we can get their signals. It will be a lot of fun, though, trying to make out what they're saying."

"It will be a good alibi, anyway," said Jimmy. "If we can't understand the dots and dashes, we can just say that they're sending in German or French or Italian. Nobody could expect us to know all those languages."

"If they did expect it, they'd be badly disappointed," said Herb. "I've been wrestling with French for three terms now, but I don't seem to know much more about it than when I started."

"I can believe that, all right," said Jimmy. "Only day before yesterday you flunked your recitation in French, and the professor told you that you were forgetting your French faster than you were learning it. He was right, wasn't he?"

"I'll say he was," said Herb, shamelessly. "At the rate I'm learning it, it would be strange if I weren't forgetting it faster. I'll have to do a lot of cramming to pass the mid-term exams."

"You fellows had better quit your talking and listen to the music," suggested Joe. "Here's a swell quartette that has just been announced. Can the chatter and do a little listening."

"That's easy," said Herb. "I'd rather hear a good quartette than almost anything else I know of."

For another hour or so they listened to the concert, which turned out to be an unusually fine one. Then, when the last selection had been given, Mr. Brandon rose to go.

"I've had a wonderful afternoon and evening," he said, "and I've enjoyed every minute of it. I hope the next time you give a party like this, Doctor Dale, that I'll be invited again."

"You surely will," replied the doctor, heartily. "The latch string always hangs outside the door for you, you know."

The radio boys also expressed their appreciation of the entertainment they had received, and Doctor Dale invited them cordially to come again.

"I'd like to be at the station to-morrow to meet Larry," he said. "But as to-morrow is Sunday, I shall be unable to get there. But don't forget to give him my congratulations on his success, will you?"

This the boys promised to do, and then they and Mr. Brandon said good-night and started homeward.

"My, but this has been a full day," said Bob. "We've certainly been moving some since this morning. And think of all we've accomplished. I'll bet Larry will get well so fast now that he'll surprise the whole lot of us."

"I'll bet Tim will be glad to hear about it,'" remarked Joe. "I wonder if he's got an engagement yet."

"He hadn't, up to a few days ago," said Bob. "Larry told me that in one of the letters he had received from him he said he had several prospects, but nothing definite. You know, of course, that Chasson wouldn't keep Tim after Larry's accident broke up the act."

"Yes, Larry told me about that," replied Joe. "I guess poor Tim has had pretty hard sledding lately, too. But he has his health, and I guess he'll land an engagement soon, if he hasn't already got one."

"He's too clever a dancer to be out of work very long, it seems to me," said Herb. "If I were manager of a show, you can bet I'd snap him up pretty quick."

"That's right," agreed Jimmy. "He's certainly a crackerjack dancer, but there is one thing about him that I never thought much of."

"What's that?" asked Bob, curiously.

"Why, haven't you ever noticed what a light appetite he has?" asked Jimmy. "I'd be ashamed of myself if I couldn't eat more than he does. He's always through a meal before I've fairly got started."

Frank Brandon laughed at this and interrupted.

"Guess I'll have to say good-night, fellows," he said. "Here's my hotel, and I, for one, feel tired enough to sleep. I'll try to be at the station to-morrow to meet Larry, but I won't promise. I'm expecting instructions from the government that may change my plans at any time."

"You don't expect to have to leave Clintonia soon, do you?" asked Bob, anxiously.

"No, I hardly think so. Not right away, anyway," answered the wireless man. "I may have to be away a few days, but I'll be back again soon."

"We're all hoping that you'll be stationed here permanently," said Bob, as all paused in front of Mr. Brandon's hotel. "We'd hate to see you transferred away from here."

"That's mighty nice to hear," said the radio expert, and his tone left no doubt that he was in earnest. "You may believe that I'll do my best to stay here, anyway. This is the center of a pretty large territory, and the wireless business is growing so fast that it's possible I'll be able to. We'll make the most of the time I'm here, anyway."

"You bet we will," said Bob. "We'll be looking for you at the station to-morrow, anyway, but if you're not there we'll tell Larry why you couldn't come."

The boys said good-night to Frank Brandon, and started on the short walk to Main Street and their homes.

<hr />

CHAPTER XVIII

NEW HOPE

"I told Larry to come on the twelve-fifty train to-morrow," said Bob. "We can get together when we come out of church, and we'll have plenty of time then to walk to the station. We don't want to take any chances of Larry's getting in without any one to meet him."

"Not on your life," agreed Joe, emphatically. "But how are we going to get him to the hotel, Bob? I know we can't get dad's car. He's too awfully busy just now. It isn't much of a walk from the station, but it's too far for Larry just yet, isn't it?"

"Let's all chip in and hire a taxi," proposed Bob. "It won't cost us much, and I guess we can all squeeze into one easily enough."

"I'm game," said Joe. "I can hang onto the spare tire if there isn't room enough inside."

"I guess that won't be necessary," laughed Bob. "Of course, Jimmy takes up a little extra room, but then Herb brings it back to average again."

It was agreed that they should hire a taxicab according to Bob's suggestion, and then the boys said "so-long" and dispersed to their homes.

The following day they met at the church door, as they had agreed, and walked rapidly down to the station. It was a glorious day, with just a hint of frost in the air, and all the boys were in high spirits. They found it hard to remember that it was Sunday and that they must act accordingly, but managed to get to the station with a due amount of decorum.

The train was a few minutes late, but the time did not seem long to them. They hired a taxicab in advance, and by the time that transaction was finished they could see the train in the distance. As it drew into the station, they eagerly scanned the alighting passengers. Larry was one of the last to alight, and the boys were almost beginning to fear that he was not on the train when they spied him on the last car. With one accord they rushed in that direction, and in a few seconds Larry found himself on the platform, with the boys bombarding him with questions and congratulations.

"How did it seem to be performing for the benefit of about half a million people at one time?" inquired Joe.

"Not very different from performing for only a few," laughed Larry. "I wasn't worrying much about the half million. What was bothering me was to please just one—Mr. Allard."

"I suppose that's about the size of it," agreed Bob, as they started toward the taxicab. "I guess he was satisfied, though, wasn't he?"

"Well, he didn't say much directly, but he took me on permanently, and is going to pay me almost twice as much as Chasson did; so I guess that's a pretty good indication that he likes the act," replied Larry. "But where are you Indians taking me to, anyway?"

"Don't ask questions, but just come along," said Bob. "We've got a taxi waiting here, and Mr. Brandon has hired a room for you at his hotel, so you see you've got nothing to worry about."

"It certainly looks that way," agreed Larry. "Well, I'm in the hands of my friends. I'll be good and do as I'm told."

"You'd better, until you get your strength back," threatened Bob. "We can lick you easily now, you know, so you'd better speak nicely to us."

"Well, when people treat me to a ride in a taxicab, I speak nicely to them anyway, so that they'll be encouraged to do it again," said Larry. "So, you see, I have a double incentive."

"You'd better make the most of this ride," laughed Joe. "When you begin to get your pay checks, we'll expect you to hire the taxicabs, shan't we, fellows?"

"You bet we will," said Jimmy. "This is the life! Taxicabs must have been made especially for me, I like to ride in them so."

"It's too bad Tim can't be with us now," said Bob. "Have you heard how he is getting along lately, Larry?"

"Oh, that reminds me!" exclaimed Larry. "You can bet your bottom dollar I've heard from him lately. Not an hour after I had gone through my act last night I got a telegram from him congratulating me. It seems that he was listening in at a radio set somewhere, and I guess it must have pretty nearly knocked him off his pins when he heard the announcer give my name. As soon as I finished he must have rushed out and sent the telegram. Here it is, and you can read it for yourselves."

He fished through his pockets, and at last produced the crumpled slip of yellow paper.

Bob took it up and read aloud.

"Fine work, old man. Keep it up. Have got engagement, too. More by letter. Tim."

"Good for him!" exclaimed Bob. "We were speaking about him last night, and wondering how he was making out. I'm mighty glad to hear that he has landed an engagement."

"So am I," said Larry. "Although, now that I've got one, he would have had half of what I made until he did drop into something. It's always been share and share alike with us."

By this time the taxicab had reached the hotel, and the boys helped Larry out. He was regaining his strength rapidly now, and his friends were delighted to note the improvement in him.

"You won't need that crutch much longer, Larry, I can see that," Bob told him.

"I hope not," responded Larry. "And won't it be a happy day when I can throw it into the discard? Believe me, it's a terrible thing to have to rely on one."

"I hope we never have to make the experiment," said Bob, soberly. "But you're mighty lucky to be getting along the way you are. When they first took you to the hospital, the doctor didn't think you'd pull through. He didn't say so in so many words, but we could see that he thought it."

"I don't doubt it," said Larry, as they slowly mounted the steps leading to the lobby. "You can believe that I felt as though the roof had caved in on top of me."

At that moment a tall boy passed them rapidly, going out of the door into the street. It was Buck Looker, and he had passed the others without recognizing them.

"Did you ever hear any more from Buck?" questioned Bob of Larry.

"No," and Larry's face clouded. "But I suppose he still thinks me guilty of that robbery."

"Forget Buck!" cried Joe. "He isn't worth worrying about."

"Perhaps not. Just the same, I wish that matter was cleared up. I hate to have a cloud over my name," answered Larry seriously.

CHAPTER XIX

LISTENING IN

Larry registered at the desk, and then they were whisked up in the elevator to the lad's room. Bob had inquired at the desk for Frank Brandon, but was informed that he had left early that morning and had left word for the boys that he would not be back in Clintonia before the following evening.

Larry's room was only two removed from that of the radio expert, and was fairly large and comfortably furnished. The young actor was delighted when he saw it.

"Say, this is great!" he exclaimed. "This has got the hospital beat a thousand ways. If the eats are only as good as the room, I'll be in clover."

"You won't find anything the matter with the eats," said Bob. "This hotel has a reputation for setting a good table, and I don't think you'll have any fault to find with it."

"When I get my first pay check, we'll try it out together," promised Larry. "You'll all be my guests, for a change, and we'll make the chef step around a bit."

"Hooray!" crowed Jimmy, "that's the kind of talk I like to hear, Larry. It certainly sounds like sweet music to me."

"It is rather pleasant," added Bob. "All you've got to do is set a date, Larry, and we'll be there with nickel-plated appetites and cast iron digestions."

"You fellows haven't said much about your radio lately. How is it coming along? I'm afraid you've spent so much time on me lately, that you've gotten behind on that new set you were telling me about."

"No, that's coming along all right," said Bob. "We haven't set any hard and fast date to have it finished, you know. We've all had to bone down pretty hard at school this term, too."

"Could you hear me plainly last evening?" inquired Larry.

"If you'd been sitting in the room with us, it couldn't have sounded any different," Joe assured him. "Doctor Dale has a good set for shorter ranges, but except under very favorable conditions he can't get the distant stations, like Detroit, for instance."

"Do you expect to be able to hear Detroit?"

"We'll be able to hear any station in the Eastern States," Bob informed him. "This is going to be a set that is a set, Larry."

"Well, so much the better," said Larry. "If you can hear as far as that, you won't have to live in fear of not hearing my performance only a few miles away. I know it would break your hearts if you couldn't."

"It makes me sad just to think of such a terrible thing," sighed Herb. "Wait till I get my handkerchief, fellows, and mop up the flowing tears."

"Aw, chase yourself," grinned Larry. "The only thing that would bother you radio bugs if you didn't hear me, would be the fear that your blamed old set wasn't working just right. You'd be down under the table fussing around with a few thousand wires, but you'd never stop to think that maybe I'd been fired by the manager, or run over by a trolley car."

"Oh, we'd never have to worry about you," said Joe. "You've heard the old saying that 'only the good die young.'"

"I certainly have," admitted Larry. "And that probably explains why that stage scenery didn't kill me outright. It's been rather a mystery to me why it didn't, but you've put me wise to the real reason."

"It will do for want of a better one, anyway,'" laughed Bob.

"If we can once get you interested in radio, Larry, you'll be as stuck on it as any of us," said Joe. "It's interesting right from the beginning, but when you dig into it a bit, it gets more fascinating all the time."

"Oh, I'm interested in radio all right, don't male any mistake about that," returned Larry, with a twinkle in his eye. "It's my meal ticket now, you know."

"Yes, but I mean in the way of recreation," persisted Joe.

"Yes, I suppose it must be mighty interesting, for a fact," admitted Larry, more seriously. "Just wait until I get strong again, and maybe I'll take it up in earnest. I've seen enough of it to realize that there are wonderful possibilities in it, anyway."

"Well, we'll be glad to initiate you any time you say the word," offered Bob. "We don't know enough about it to keep us awake at night, but we can probably explain a few things to you."

"Oh, I'll ask questions until you wish you'd never mentioned radio to me," laughed Larry. "If I do take it up, I'll have to start at the beginning."

"That's where most everybody starts," announced Jimmy. "You won't be a bit worse off than we were, will he, fellows?"

"I should say not," answered Bob. "When we started, we hardly knew the difference between an antenna and a ground wire. We had our own troubles at first; and we're still having them, as far as that goes. There always seems to be something new coming up that you have to work out."

"If I keep on getting good pay from the broadcasting station, I'll be able to buy a set, anyway," said Larry. "What's the use of working so hard over one, when you can buy them all made up? All you have to do is hook them up to a small antenna, and you get your music right off the bat."

But the radio boys all scouted this idea.

"Of course you can buy one all made up," said Bob. "But there's not half the fun in operating that kind of set as there is in one that you've made yourself. And besides, you can get a lot better results when you've made the thing yourself and understand just what's in it and how it works. If you don't get good results some evening, you know where to look for the trouble."

"It's like driving an automobile when you don't understand the mechanism," added Joe. "As long as everything goes all right you go sailing along, but let something go wrong, and you're up a tree right away. You haven't any idea of where to look for the trouble."

"All right, all right," laughed Larry. "Don't shoot, and I'll promise never to mention it again."

"See that you keep it, then," said Bob, laughing. "But anybody who buys a made-up set isn't entitled to be called a real radio fan; at least, we don't think so."

"I suppose you're right," agreed Larry. "It must be half the fun of the game when you do the job yourself. But remember that everybody can't build elaborate sets the way you fellows do, even if they want to. They haven't got the knack."

"I suppose that's so," conceded Bob. "But almost anybody that can drive a nail straight can do it. It's mostly a matter of hard work and a little study."

"Well, when I get a little stronger, maybe I'll take a fling at it," said Larry. "But just at present, the only thing I can think about is getting something to eat. I had a pretty early breakfast, and now I'm rather anxious to try some of that good cooking you tell me this hotel is famous for."

"My!" exclaimed Bob, jumping to his feet. "I'm glad you mentioned dinner, Larry. I'll have to take it on the run if I'm going to get home in time for dinner. They're always sore if I'm late, too."

"And to think that I overlooked such an important thing as Sunday dinner!" ejaculated Jimmy, searching frantically around for his cap. "I only hope I can last out until I get home," he went on. "If I do, it will only be on account of my strong will power. I'm afraid poor old Herb hasn't much chance to pull through."

"Huh!" snorted Herb. "If you had to depend on will power to get you home, you'd never get a block away from here. You'll get home all right, but the thing that gets you there will be the thought of how good the chicken and apple pie are going to taste."

"Well, nobody could have a stronger motive than that, after all," said Jimmy. "Confound this elevator, anyway. I guess it's never going to come up. You fellows can wait if you want to, but I'm going to walk down. I know I'll get there, then."

"Doughnuts does have a good idea once in a while," said Joe. "I'll do the same thing." The others were nothing loath, so they shook hands with Larry and clattered down the long flights of stairs at high speed, for, as Bob said, it would never do to let the elevator beat them down after all.

CHAPTER XX

THE WONDERFUL SCIENCE

The boys arrived at the street floor breathless but triumphant, and started in the direction of home at so brisk a pace that poor Jimmy had some difficulty in keeping up. He was in as much of a hurry as any of the others, however, and by great effort managed to keep up with his companions.

"After this, we all should be eligible to go in a walking race," laughed Bob, as they paused a minute at his door. "Can you all get around this evening and listen to some radio? I've got to get out some lessons this afternoon, and I guess you have, too."

"I should say so!" exclaimed Joe. "You know how much chance we had to do them yesterday, and I've got a good three hours' work ahead of me. I guess I can get around this evening all right, though."

Herb and Jimmy both said that they would be on hand, and then they went on, separating as each reached his own home.

Shortly after supper that evening they all met at the Layton home according to appointment. As it was Sunday, they did not do any work on their new set, but the whole Layton family gathered around the loud speaker that evening, as a prominent preacher was to deliver a sermon by radio, and they were all eager to hear it.

Before the sermon there was an organ recital, and they heard this perfectly, after the boys had succeeded in tuning out one or two amateurs who sometimes made them trouble. Of course, everybody enjoyed the recital, and also the sermon, which was delivered in very effective style.

"This is certainly being up to date," commented Mr. Layton, when the sermon was over. "When I was the same age as you boys, I was expected to be in church every Sunday evening without fail. But now it does not seem quite so necessary, when it is possible to have religious services right in the home, as we have had them this evening. I think the Layton family is indebted to you boys, as the chances are neither Mrs. Layton nor I would ever have become interested in it if Bob and you hadn't introduced us to it."

"I'll bet you never thought much of it when we first started to build an amateur set, now did you, Dad?" accused Bob.

"As I don't see any way out of it, I suppose I'll have to confess that you're right," laughed Mr. Layton. "But you must remember that you boys were among the first to take up wireless in Clintonia, and at that time nobody in town had thought anything about it. I guess we didn't realize its possibilities."

"It was a surprise to me when that first set that you boys made really worked," admitted Mrs. Layton. "I remember that it sounded very nice right from the start, too."

"Yes, that was a good old set," said Bob. "It didn't satisfy us for long, though. It was all right under favorable conditions, but you couldn't do much tuning with it."

"Not only that, but the range was pretty limited, too," chimed in Joe. "When I think of all the planning we had to do before we got it made, I feel like laughing."

"It was no laughing matter then, though," said Herb. "If it hadn't worked, we'd have been a pretty disappointed crowd."

"I'll never forget the sensation when that first music came in over our set," said Bob. "It was certainly a grand and glorious feeling. I only hope our new set comes up to scratch as well as that one did."

"I guess there isn't much doubt about the new set," observed Joe, confidently. "It will just *have* to work."

"Look out," laughed Mr. Layton. "Don't forget the old saying, that 'pride goeth before a fall.'"

"Yes, we may have an awful bump coming to us, I suppose," said Joe. "But we'd be awfully sore if it didn't work, after all the labor we've put on it."

"We'll make it work, all right," predicted Bob. "Maybe not on the very first trial, but we'll get it going in the end, I'll bet a cookie."

"I surely hope it will be all right, because I know how bad you would all feel if it didn't," said Mrs. Layton. "I never knew boys would work so hard at anything, just for the sake of the fun they expect to get out of it."

"They may get a good deal more than just fun out of it," remarked Mr. Layton, seriously. "It looks to me as though radiophony were only just starting at present, and it seems certain that it offers a big field for any one who has the desire and ability to take up that line of work. It may turn out to be a fine thing for them later on."

"I suppose that's very true," said his wife, thoughtfully. "Although that side of it never occurred to me before."

After a little further conversation, Joe, Herb, and Jimmy said good-night and took their leave, thinking, as they walked home, of what Mr. Layton had said.

They had all entertained the same idea before, but his words had encouraged them. Why not? Surely there must be many openings in so large a field for bright and ambitious young fellows, and in their dreams that night the boys had visions of fame and fortune attained through the medium of wireless telephony.

They were discussing this the next afternoon on their way home from school, when their speculations were brought to an abrupt end by the sight of Larry hobbling down the street toward them as fast as he could travel with his crutch, his face flushed and his free arm wildly waving.

CHAPTER XXI

THE VANISHING CROOKS

The radio boys broke into a run, and soon reached their excited friend.

"What's the matter, Larry?" asked Bob. "You look as though you had just seen a ghost. What's the trouble?"

"I wish you'd gotten here a few minutes sooner!" panted Larry. "Confound this blamed crutch of mine. How can anybody hope to make any speed with one of these things?"

"He can't," said Bob. "But hurry up and tell us what's eating you."

"I just saw the fellows that were in that motor boat when it ran us down!" exclaimed Larry.

"You did?" cried the radio boys in chorus. "Did you try to stop them?"

"Of course I did," replied Larry. "But they evidently recognized me, for they gave me one look, and then started off at top speed. I tried to run after them, but I'm too blamed crippled yet to do much speeding, and of course they got away clean. If you fellows had come along three minutes sooner, we could have caught them, I think."

"They can't have got very far yet, then," said Bob. "Which way did they go? It may not be too late to catch them even now."

"They went around that corner," answered Larry, pointing with his crutch. "I got there as soon as I could, but by the time I arrived there was no sign of them."

"I'm afraid we haven't much chance to catch them now, but we might as well try, anyway," said Bob. "Judging from the direction they took, it looks as though they might have headed for the station. Suppose we each take a different street, and work down to the station, keeping our eyes open as we go along? Even if we don't succeed in catching them, we may find somebody who knows them and can give us some information."

"Sounds good to me," agreed Joe, briefly, and the others also assented to Bob's plan.

"I'll go straight down High Street, then," said Bob, decisively. "You take Jerome Avenue, Joe. You take Van Ness Avenue, Herb. And you take Southern Boulevard, Jimmy. They all run together near the station, and we can meet there.

So-long, Larry. Whether we learn anything or not, we'll come back to the hotel and let you know all about it."

"All right, then, I'll be waiting for you," said Larry, with a wave of his hand. "I only wish that I could help you, but I'm a lame horse yet. Good luck, anyway."

The radio boys set out at top speed, each one hunting high and low along the street assigned to him, and asking questions of every one he met. But the strangers seemed to have vanished into thin air, for, hunt as they would, the boys could find no trace of them. At the railroad station they learned that a train had left for New York only a few minutes before, but the ticket agent said he did not remember selling tickets to any men such as the boys described.

"That doesn't prove anything, though," he said, as he noted their disappointment. "I sell so many tickets here during the day that I don't notice who buys them much. The only time I'd be likely to notice anything would be if the parties were excited or nervous, and I don't remember anything like that this afternoon."

The boys thanked him, and left the station.

"That's too bad," said Bob. "I would have given a lot to have caught those fellows for Larry. People that are mean and selfish enough to upset a boat and then not even try to rescue the people in it, ought to get what's coming to them."

"I'd certainly have enjoyed taking a swift punch or two at them myself," agreed Joe.

"Well, if we didn't catch them, it wasn't for lack of trying," said Herb. "People looked at me as though they thought I was crazy when I asked them questions about the fellows we were after. I didn't even know enough about them to describe them."

"My idea was that they'd probably keep on running even after they'd gotten away from Larry, and in that case somebody would have been sure to notice them," explained Bob. "It looks as though they were wise enough to slow down as soon as they thought they were safely away, though."

"No use crying over spilt milk," said Jimmy philosophically. "Let's go back to Larry and report 'nothing doing.'"

"I suppose that's about all we can do," agreed Bob. "We'll keep a sharp lookout on the way back, and we may find something, after all."

But this hope was doomed to disappointment. There was no sign of the rascals they sought, and there was no help for it but to tell Larry of their lack of success.

The latter was naturally greatly disappointed, but he put a cheerful face on the matter.

"When they once got away from me, I gave up hope of catching them, for this time, anyway," he said. "Clintonia is getting to be such a big town that it's easy for people to lose themselves in it. The only thing to do is hope for better luck next time. I'm mighty grateful to you fellows for trying so hard to find them, too."

"Don't thank us for doing nothing," said Bob, a little ruefully. "If we had caught those rascals, it would have been different."

"Oh, it was just hard luck that you fellows didn't come along a few minutes sooner. We'd have got them then, sure. But I've got a hunch that we'll run across them again."

"I'll bet you traveled faster with that stick of yours than you ever thought you could, didn't you?" asked Herb, with a grin.

"I guess I did," laughed Larry. "I must have looked funny hopping along there. But it won't be long now before I'll be traveling around on my own two feet again."

"You're certainly looking better every time I see you," remarked Bob. "I guess you'll be plenty strong enough to start in at steady work at the broadcasting station next week, won't you?"

"Oh, sure," responded Larry. "I could do it this week, as far as that goes."

"Don't get too ambitious," said Joe. "A week's rest here will do you all kinds of good."

"Do you find the grub as good as we told you it would be?" asked Jimmy.

"It's simply heavenly," said Larry, solemnly.

"Say!" exclaimed Bob, suddenly, "have any of you Indians happened to think what next Monday is?"

"Sure," said Herb, flippantly. "It's the day after next Sunday. Ask me something harder next time."

"That's right," said Bob, giving him a withering glance. "As our friend Herbert says, it is the day after Sunday, but it also happens to be Columbus Day, and therefore a holiday. How did we ever come to forget that?"

"Hooray!" they shouted, and with one accord linked arms and executed an impromptu dance.

"That being so, let's go with Larry when he reports for work," proposed Joe. "Who's game to do it?"

"I'm with you!" exclaimed Bob. "We can see that Larry gets there all right, and maybe Mr. Allard will show us over the station. We were in such a hurry when we were there before that we couldn't see very much."

"I'd like to go first rate," said Herb. "But I'm so far behind on my French that I'm afraid I'll have to stay at home and make up for lost time. I'm 'way back in math., too."

"I won't be able to go either, I'm afraid," said Jimmy, dolefully. "Dad has just taken a big contract, and I've promised to help him all my spare time next week. I'd forgotten about Monday being a holiday, though," he added, truthfully.

"Well, if you can't, that's all there is to it," said Bob. "Maybe you'll change your minds before then, though."

"I don't want you to come just on my account, fellows," said Larry. "Of course, I'd love to have you come, but I don't want you to think you've got to."

"It isn't that at all," Bob assured him. "In the first place, it will be fun to take the trip, and then, if we get a chance to look around the station, we may get some good tips for our new set."

"Well," said Larry, doubtfully, "since you put it that way, it will be great to have you come with me. I guess I've got influence enough around there already to show you the inside works."

"All right, then, we'll consider that settled," said Bob. "Joe and I will call for you early in the afternoon. By that time Mr. Brandon will be back, and maybe he'll come, too."

The radio inspector returned the next day, but he could not promise to accompany the little party, as he had to attend a meeting at headquarters the following Monday.

CHAPTER XXII

BROADCASTING MARVELS

The remainder of the week sped quickly by, and almost before the boys realized it the holiday had arrived. Larry spent the morning at Bob's house, where he watched Bob and Joe working on the new set, and kept his promise to ask questions.

"It doesn't do me much good, though," he said, fairly puzzled at last. "That's about the most mysterious looking box of tricks that I've ever had the hard luck to look at. What are all those dials and knobs for? Do you keep your money in there, or what?"

"You must think they are combination locks," laughed Bob. "This knob here controls a condenser, and this one a transformer."

"But how do you know what to do with them?" asked the bewildered Larry. "How do you know which one to turn and which one to leave alone?"

"You don't," laughed Bob. "You may have an idea about where they should be placed, but it's different every evening."

"Yes, and during the evening, too," added Joe. "You have to keep adjusting all the time to get the best results."

"Well, if it depended on me, I'm afraid I'd only get the worst results," said Larry. "It all looks terribly complicated to me."

"You don't have to worry much about it, anyway," said Joe. "All you have to do is whistle into the transmitter, and it's up to us to hear you. We have to do all the work."

"It's a lucky thing for me that it is that way," said Larry. "If I had to learn all about radio before I could give my act, I'd probably starve to death first."

"Radio is just like everything else," said Bob. "It looks very mysterious and difficult to an outsider, but when you get into it a little way and understand the rudiments, it begins to look a lot simpler. It wouldn't take you very long to catch on to it. Especially a smart lad like you," he added, with a grin.

"Cut out the comedy," said Larry. "Any time I get a compliment from you or Joe, I know there's a nigger in the woodpile somewhere."

"The trouble with you is, you're too modest," said Joe. "When we do say something good about you, you think we're only kidding."

"I don't think—I know," replied Larry, grinning. "I suppose, though, that radio must be pretty easy, or you fellows wouldn't know so much about it."

"That remark has all the appearance of a dirty dig," said Bob. "But I suppose we can't land on him until he gets entirely well, can we, Joe?"

"No, let him live a little while longer," replied his friend. "We'll get even for that knock, though, Larry, my boy."

"I won't lie awake at night worrying about it, anyway," replied Larry. "But I'm not going to interfere with your work any more. Just go ahead as though I weren't here, and I'll try to learn something by watching what you do."

Bob and Joe worked steadily then until Mrs. Layton called to them to come up to lunch.

"Toot! toot!" went Larry, imitating faithfully a factory whistle blowing for twelve o'clock. "Time to knock off, you laborers. If you work any longer I won't let you belong to the union any more."

"No danger of that," said Bob. "I've been feeling hungry ever since ten o'clock, so I'm not going to lose any time now. Come on up and we'll see what mother's got for us."

They found a lunch waiting for them that would have made a dyspeptic hungry, and they attacked it in a workmanlike manner that drew an approving comment from Mrs. Layton.

"I declare it's some satisfaction to get a meal for you boys," she declared. "You certainly eat as though you enjoyed it."

"There's no camouflage about that, Mother; we *do* enjoy it," answered Bob.

"We wouldn't be human if we didn't enjoy it, that's fairly certain," said Larry. "The meals at the hotel are pretty good, but they're not in the same class with this lunch at all."

"I know they have a reputation for setting a good table there," said Mrs. Layton. "I hope you fare as well in the city. You'll board there, I suppose, won't you?"

"Yes, I expect to," said Larry. "Mr. Allard, the manager, recommended me to a good place near the station, and I guess they won't let me starve to death there."

"Let us hope not," smiled Mrs. Layton. "Any time you are in Clintonia, we'd be very glad to have you visit us, you know. I suppose Bob has told you that, though."

"I certainly did!" exclaimed her son. "I have a hunch that after eating a while in boarding houses a good home-cooked meal must be a welcome change."

"I'll say it is," assented Larry. "But there are one or two good restaurants fairly near the station, anyway, so in case I get tired of the food at the boarding house, I can switch to a restaurant for a while."

"That sounds like jumping from the frying pan into the fire," grinned Joe.

"I suppose it is something along that line," assented Larry, with a rueful laugh. "But what is a poor fellow to do?"

"I suppose it can't be helped," assented Bob, as he finished his dessert. "But now, fellows, there doesn't seem to be anything more to eat, so I guess we'd better be moving if we're going to catch the two o'clock train."

"That shows you how much gratitude I can expect from him," said Mrs. Layton, laughingly appealing to the others. "'Eat and run' seems to be his motto these days."

"Well, there's always so much to be done, it would keep anybody on the jump," protested Bob. "I don't seem to be fading away under the strain, though, do I?"

"No. And while your appetite continues the way it is, I guess I shan't need to worry about you," replied Mrs. Layton.

Larry and Joe said good-by to their hostess, and then all three boys started for the station. They had good fortune in catching the trolley that ran to the railroad station, and just had time to get their tickets before the train pulled in.

It was more than a two-hours' run to the point where they must change cars, but it seemed to them that they had hardly gotten settled in their seats before it was time to get off. Larry told them many comical stories of his experiences while traveling from town to town and funny incidents that had occurred at rehearsals and during performances.

"You get pretty tired of traveling all the time, though," Larry remarked at length. "This engagement you fellows and Mr. Brandon have gotten for me is certainly a relief. I'd be mighty glad to have it, even if I hadn't been hurt. I've had enough of jumping around all over the country to suit me for a while."

"I'll bet it does get mighty tiresome," assented Bob, as the boys rose to get out. "But here we are, and as the train doesn't go any further, I suppose we might as well get off."

"That isn't a bad idea," said Joe. "I suppose there's no use trying to persuade the conductor to go on a little further."

"I don't imagine you'd better even think of it," said Larry. "I've got a hunch that he'd only get peeved if you did."

"Well, then, I'll take your advice," grinned Joe.

As they emerged from the terminal into the street at their final destination, Joe asked:

"But how are we going to find this place, Larry? Do you know the way?"

"No, but I know how to find somebody who does," replied Larry, and he signaled to a taxicab driver.

"Nix, Larry, nix!" expostulated Bob. "We can get there on the trolleys. You'd better save your cash."

"You fellows blew me to a taxi ride when I landed in Clintonia the last time, so I'm going to do the same for you," said Larry, obstinately. "No use in kicking now, so just forget it."

During this brief dialogue the taxi had approached them, and now stopped as the driver swung open the door.

"Hop in, fellows," directed Larry, and then he gave the driver directions to drive to the big broadcasting station.

With a jerk and a rattle they were off, and there ensued an exciting ten minutes as the taxicab scooted through the traffic, shooting across streets, and missing collisions by the narrowest of margins a dozen times in the course of the brief journey. The boys held on tight to prevent being thrown from their seats, and they all heaved sighs of relief when at length the vehicle came to a sudden halt in front of the big broadcasting station.

"Whew!" exclaimed Bob. "I don't know what this will cost you, Larry, but whatever it is, you get your money's worth of excitement, anyway. Taking a ride in one of those things is like going out to commit suicide."

"That's nothin'," grinned the driver, who had overheard this remark. "We was takin' it easy all de way. If you guys had been in a hurry, now, I might have shown you a little speed."

"Well, you did pretty well, as it was," said Bob. "You were in a hurry, if we weren't."

Larry paid the man, and he was off at top speed and had disappeared around a corner before Larry had fairly put his change away.

"That must be a great life, driving a taxi all day in a big city," said Larry. "But let's go in, and see if we can find the boss. I hope he'll act tip nice and show you fellows the whole works. I'll go around with you and try to look wise, but I won't have any idea of what it's all about."

Entering the office, they had little difficulty in seeing the manager, and he readily consented to have the boys look over the station, turning them over to an assistant, as he was too busy to take them around himself.

Mr. Reed, the assistant, did not appear particularly pleased with his assignment at first, but when he found that the boys were well grounded in radio, his attitude changed.

"I get tired of showing people around who don't know a thing about radio, and do nothing but ask fool questions," he explained. "But when I get some one who knows the subject and can understand what I'm showing him, that's a different matter."

He showed them over the sending station from the studio to the roof. The boys listened with the keenest interest as he described to them the methods by which the broadcasting was carried on, which every night delighted hundreds of thousands of people within range of the station.

In a little room close to the roof they saw the sending apparatus which really did the work. There was a series of five vacuum bulbs through which the current passed, receiving a vastly greater amplification from each, until from the final one it climbed into the antenna and was flung into space. To the casual onlooker they would have seemed like simply so many ordinary electric bulbs arranged in a row and glowing with, perhaps, unusual brilliance.

But the boys knew that they were vastly more than this. Where the electric light tube would have contained only the filament, these tubes at which they were looking contained also a plate and a grid—the latter being that magical invention which had worked a complete revolution in the science of radio and had made broadcasting possible. From the heated filament electrons were shot off in a stream toward the plate, and by the wonder-working intervention of the grid were amplified immeasurably in power and then passed on to the other tube, which in turn passed it on to a third, and so on until the sound that had started as the ordinary tone of a human voice had been magnified many thousands of times. This little series of tubes was able to make the crawl of a fly sound like the tread of an elephant and there is no doubt that a time will come when through this agency the drop of a pin in New York City can be heard in San Francisco.

The boys were so fascinated with the possibilities contained in the apparatus that it was only with reluctance that they left the roof and went to the studio. This they found to be a long, rather narrow room, wholly without windows, and with the floors covered with the heaviest of rugs. The reason for this, as their guide explained, was to shut out all possible sound except that which it was desired to transmit over the radio.

"What is the idea of having no windows?" asked Bob.

"So there shall be no vibration from the window panes," replied Mr. Reed. "I tell you, boys, this broadcasting hasn't been a matter of days, but is the development of months of the hardest kind of work and experiment. We have had to test, reject, and sift all possible suggestions in order to reach perfection. I don't mean by that to say that we have reached it yet, but we're on the way. New problems are coming up all the time, and we are kept busy trying to solve them.

"It seems a simple thing," he went on, "to talk or sing into that microphone," pointing to a little disk-like instrument about the height of a man's head. "But even there the least miscalculation may wholly spoil the effect of the speech or the music. Now, in a theater, the actor is at least twenty feet or so from the nearest of his audience and the sounds that he makes in drawing in his breath are not perceptible. If he stayed too close to the microphone, however, that drawing in of breath, or some other little peculiarity of his delivery, would be so plainly heard that it would interfere with the effect of his performance. So, with certain instruments. A flute, for instance, has no mechanical stops, so a flute player can stand comparatively near the microphone. The player of a cornet, however, must stand some distance back or else the clicking of the stops of his instrument will interfere with his music. These are only a few of the difficulties that we meet and have to guard against. There are dozens of others that require just as much vigilance to guard against in order to get a perfect performance. It's a pleasure to explain these things to you, boys, for you catch on quickly."

"We're a long way from being experts," said Bob, "but we've done quite a good deal of radio work and built several sets of our own, so we can at least ask intelligent questions."

"Well, fire away, and I'll try to answer them," replied Mr. Reed. "You may be able to stick me, though."

He said this as a joke, but before they had completed a tour of the building the boys had asked him some posers that he was at a loss to answer.

"I almost think you fellows should be taking me around," he said at last. "Blamed if I don't think you know as much as I do about it."

CHAPTER XXIII

THE FIRST VENTURE

"They're regular sharks, those boys," said Larry, who was thoroughly enjoying Mr. Reed's discomfiture. "I think they'd be able to stick Mr. Edison, I'll be blest if I don't."

"Nonsense," laughed Bob. "We're only asking about things we don't understand ourselves. You know the did saying, 'a fool can ask more questions than a wise man can answer.'"

"Hey, there, speak for yourself!" exclaimed Joe. "You may be a fool, but don't class me under that heading."

"I was only speaking figuratively, as the profs say," laughed Bob. "I don't want you to take me too literally, of course."

"All I've got to say is, that you're both pretty well up on radio," said Mr. Reed. "Are you a shark too, Larry?"

"Not I," answered Larry. "I've been trying to learn something about it since I met Bob and Joe here, but I can't say that I've made much progress. Besides, you can't do much learning in a hospital," he added, with a rueful laugh.

"It isn't what you would call an ideal place," admitted Mr. Reed. "But now that you're working here, you ought to pick it up pretty soon."

"I'm going to make a real try at it now," promised Larry. "It's a shame to be so ignorant about the business that's giving you a living."

"Yes, but I don't see where our knowledge of radio is bringing us much cash," said Joe.

"How about that hundred and fifty dollars we won between us in prizes?" Bob reminded him. "That was quite a little cash, wasn't it?"

"That's a long time ago, though," returned Joe. "I wish I knew some way to pick up a little extra change now. Christmas is not very far off, and heaven knows how I'm going to buy anybody any present."

"Can you do anything in the way of a song or a recitation?" asked Mr. Reed. "I know Mr. Allard needs one or two short bits to fill out the programme to-night, but I don't suppose you could do anything of that sort, could you?"

81

"I'm afraid not," replied Joe. "I know two or three recitations that I learned for the elocution class, but I'm afraid that's about the full extent of my entertaining power. If I tried to sing, folks would think that some accident had happened to their apparatus."

"A good recitation or two might be just what the boss is looking for," returned Mr. Reed. "It Couldn't do any harm to ask him about it, anyway. What is your specialty, Layton?"

"There's no such thing," laughed Bob. "As an entertainer, I'd be a terrible frost."

"I'm not so sure of that," said the other. "Suppose we look up Mr. Allard, anyway, and see what he has to say."

"I'll try anything once," said Bob. "I suppose it can't do any harm to try, anyway."

"If you can get away with it, why not pick up a few dollars?" asked Larry. "It isn't like facing a big audience, you know. The audience is there, all right, but you don't see them, and it's easier to forget about them than in a theater."

"I wouldn't try it for a farm in a theater," said Joe. "But I guess I could work up nerve enough to talk into that sending apparatus. It won't be as bad as reciting in the auditorium at high school, at any rate."

"Don't bank too much on it," warned their conductor. "Mr. Allard may not think well of the plan, or he may have found some one else by this time."

"I'll be satisfied either way," said Bob, philosophically. "I'd like to make a little money, all right; but, on the other hand, I'm beginning to get stage fright already. If Mr. Allard turns us down it will be a relief, after all."

But the manager, when interviewed, seemed relieved at the prospect of having their services.

"I think I can use you both very nicely this evening," he said. "Of course, I'll have to hear your stuff before I can tell. Suppose you let us hear one or two of your recitations, Mr. Atwood."

"All right," grinned Joe. "You'll probably give me the hook before I get through, though; but you can't say I didn't warn you."

"We'll take a chance," smiled the manager. "Do your worst."

Thus exhorted, Joe recited a humorous piece he had learned recently for delivery in the elocution class, and he recited it very well, too. When he had finished Mr. Allard called for more, and Joe obliged with the only other selection in his repertoire.

"That's first rate," said the manager, when he had finished. "I think that ought to go all right. I think I'll give you ten or fifteen minutes on the bill. Now, how about you, Mr. Layton? What's your specialty?"

"I don't own such a thing," grinned Bob. "I know one piece that I learned for elocution, the same as Joe, but you wouldn't want two of the same variety on the bill."

"No, that's true," agreed Mr. Allard. "Let's see, now," and he thought a minute or two.

"How would this do?" he exclaimed at length. "We've got all sorts of books here with jokes and riddles in them. Suppose we pick out a few good conundrums, and you can learn them and the answers between now and seven o'clock. Then, right at the beginning of the bedtime stuff, you give the riddles, and we'll announce that the answers aren't to be given until the very end of the performance. That will keep them guessing all through it, and keep them interested. Then at the end you can give the answers. How does that strike you?"

"I'm game," replied Bob, grinning. "I guess if I bone down to it I can learn a few by then."

"You won't even have to memorize them, if you don't want to," said Mr. Allard. "You can read them right off if you'd rather. Your audience won't be able to see what you're doing, you know."

"That would probably be better," agreed Bob. "Then there won't be any chance of my forgetting the answers. Think of how tough it would be on the kids if I gave them a riddle and then forgot the answer. That would be a terrible trick to play on them."

"Well, you can suit yourself about that," returned Mr. Allard. "It's almost six o'clock now, so perhaps you'd better go out and get a bite to eat right now. I'll pick out a few good conundrums, and you'd better get back as soon as you can and study them up a bit."

"All right," said Bob. "We'll make it snappy."

He and Joe and Larry went out and had a quick meal at the nearest restaurant.

"You fellows have broken into the entertaining game with your usual speed," remarked Larry. "Who would have imagined this morning that you would be on the broadcasting programme this evening?"

"We wouldn't have been, one time out of a hundred," answered Bob. "If one of the regulars hadn't been sick, we never would have gotten a look in."

"'It's an ill wind that blows nobody any good,'" quoted Joe. "We'll make our car fare out of this, and something over. It's lucky I happened to speak as I did to Mr. Reed."

"But say!" exclaimed Bob, struck by a sudden thought. "Won't Jimmy and Herb be knocked silly when they hear our voices this evening? They won't be able to believe their ears."

"You said it," declared Joe. "But the worst of it is, we won't be there to see their faces at the time. I'd give the evening's profits to see them then."

"It will be a scream, all right," agreed Larry, with a chuckle. "You two will have it all over all the other radio fans in Clintonia when you get back. They'll be green with envy."

"I guess it will make them sit up and take notice," assented Bob. "Just make out Lon Beardsley won't be sore. This will be a terrible blow to him."

"It's a good thing it isn't the other way around," said Joe. "If it were Lon who was on the broadcasting programme, we'd never hear the last of it. You'd be hearing about it ten years from now."

The three friends finished their meal and returned to the broadcasting station, where Mr. Allard was waiting for Bob with the riddles that he had selected.

"Here are a few funny ones," he said. "You can practice up on the delivery of them, and Larry will give you some pointers about the best way to say them. I don't imagine you'll have any trouble when the time comes."

CHAPTER XXIV

WINNING OUT

"It seems to me he takes a lot for granted," said Bob, after the manager had left the room. "How does he know that both of us won't get rattled right in the middle of the thing and ball up the whole programme?"

"I guess it's because he's heard something about both you and Joe from Mr. Brandon, and he's pretty sure you'll come up to the scratch," said Larry. "That's the way I figure it out, anyway."

"Well, we'll do the best we can to live up to our reputation, if that's the case," said Bob. "I'll read these things aloud the way I think they should go, Larry, and you correct me if I'm wrong."

"Go ahead," replied Larry. "You've been telling me so much about radio that I ought to be willing to tell you something about how to put a joke over."

Bob settled down to his task in earnest then, and for an hour rehearsed the jokes with Larry, who drilled him in the most effective way to tell them to advantage.

"There!" exclaimed Larry, at the end of that time. "I think you ought to get by all right now, Bob. You're doing fine."

"Well, if they don't like me, I can't help it," said Bob. "At any rate, they won't be able to throw any dead cats at me. That's one big advantage that radio entertainers have."

"That's true enough," laughed Larry, "although I hadn't thought about it before. Maybe I'd have had a poor pussy cat wrapped about my neck before this if I'd been doing my act in a regular theater."

"Nonsense!" replied Bob. "Nobody threw anything at you when you were acting in a regular theater, did he?"

"No," admitted Larry. "That is, nothing except big bunches of American Beauty roses," he hastily added.

"Oh, of course, that's understood," gibed Joe. "I suppose you had to hire a big truck every evening to cart them away."

"Yes, every evening," grinned Larry. "And the applause——good gracious! The people for blocks around used to complain about it."

"You don't get much applause now," laughed Bob. "How does it seem to perform for the benefit of a telephone transmitter instead of an audience?"

"It never bothered me much," replied Larry. "It seems to be pretty hard for some of the actors, though, especially the comedians. When they spring a funny joke they're used to hearing their audience laugh, and when they don't hear anything, they get peeved sometimes. They can't get used to the blank silence after their best efforts."

"I can easily understand how it would have that effect," said Bob. "It might save them a lot of trouble, though. Take the case of a black-face artist. He wouldn't need to put on any make-up at all, if he didn't want to."

"But if they don't, they don't feel natural, and it's apt to spoil their act. An actor is pretty temperamental, you know."

"Well, I'm beginning to feel that way myself," sighed Joe. "I wish it were time for us to spring our stuff on an unsuspecting public and get it over with. It must be pretty near time for the first number now, isn't it?"

"It sure is," answered Larry. "We'd better go on up to the transmitting room. The worst crime a public performer can commit is to be late, you know."

"And to think that I'm the poor fellow that's supposed to open the show!" exclaimed Bob.

"My, I'll be as glad to get it over with as you will, Joe."

"That's saying a mouthful," replied his friend. "Oh, what a relief it will be!"

"If the audience can stand it, you two ought to be able to," said Larry, cruelly. "Quit your worrying."

"I guess if the audience can stand you, it won't mind us," returned Bob, giving Larry a friendly poke in the ribs. "Guess that will hold you a little while, old timer."

Before Larry could think of a suitable retort they had entered the transmitting room, and he had to postpone his reply for the time being.

Mr. Allard was already there.

"How do you feel?" he asked them, in greeting. "Probably a trifle nervous?"

"Just a little bit," Bob admitted. "I think we'll make out all right, though."

"Good!" replied the manager. "Don't get rattled, and you'll go over all right. From what Mr. Brandon has told me, you don't either of you rattle easily, though."

"We're ready any time you are, sir," was Bob's comment.

"All right, then," said Mr. Allard, crisply. "It's time now, Morton," addressing the announcer. "You can go ahead and announce Layton's act."

This the announcer did, and then, tense with excitement but thoroughly master of himself, Bob stepped to the transmitter and propounded the first of his conundrums. With book in hand, Larry stood at his elbow to prompt him in case he forgot anything, but his friendly services were not needed. Bob went through the whole list without a mistake and with no fumbling, speaking clearly and distinctly into the transmitter. Although he could not see his audience, he nevertheless sensed the listening thousands, and felt the lift and exhilaration that come to the successful entertainer. His part in the programme was short, a scant ten minutes, but he enjoyed every minute of it.

When he had asked the last riddle, he stepped back, and mopped big drops of perspiration from his face.

"Whew!" he exclaimed. "I'm glad that's over, although it wasn't as bad as I thought it would be."

"You've got to go all through it again when you give the answers," Larry reminded him, cruelly.

"I guess I can stand it," said Bob. "Did I do it all right?"

"Sure you did," they all assured him. "It was good work."

In a little while the time came for Joe to give his recitations, and he, too, did good work. It was easy to see that the manager was pleased with both of them, and, indeed, he did not hesitate to say so.

"If you fellows didn't live so far away, I'd be glad to make you a regular part of the programme," he told them later. "You both have a good delivery, and I can see that Brandon was right when he said you didn't lack nerve. It's too bad you don't live in this town."

"I don't think we could do much along that line just now, anyway," said Bob, much pleased. "Between high school and building radio sets we don't have much time left over. We appreciate your giving us a chance on the bill to-night, though. We never dreamed of such a thing when we left the house this morning."

"I can't wait to get back to Clintonia to see what Herb and Jimmy have to say," remarked Joe. "I'll bet their eyes are sticking out now like a crab's."

The boys then said good-night to Mr. Allard and Larry, and took a somewhat hurried departure, as they had very little time left in which to make the last train for Clintonia.

Meantime, Herb and Jimmy had been treated to the surprise of their lives. Shortly after supper Jimmy had whistled the familiar call in front of Herb's house, and when his friend had emerged had invited him to come to his house that evening.

"You know I've got my set rigged up now," he said, "the one that I entered for the Ferberton prize. It didn't win the prize, but it's a pretty good set all the same. There's a good radio programme on for this evening, and I suppose you want to hear it as much as I do."

"Yes, I certainly do," answered Herb. "Besides, if we hear Larry, we'll know that the three of them arrived at the other end on time. It will be almost as good as having them right here with us."

"Get your coat on, then, and we'll be going," said Jimmy. "It's not so far from seven o'clock, now."

Herb ran back into the house, and, emerging shortly afterward, joined his friend, and they set out for Jimmy's house.

"Conditions ought to be ideal for radio to-night," Herb remarked, as they walked along. "It's clear as a bell. There won't be enough static to-night to bother any one."

"So much the better," said Jimmy. "That set of mine doesn't get very good results when the static is bad. I thought it was the real thing once, but compared with the sets we've made since, I can see where it might be a lot better."

"Well, there aren't many things that are so good that they can't be improved," remarked Herb. "I suppose even if I set out to make a perfect set, I might fall a little short of the mark somewhere."

"That seems almost impossible, but of course you ought to know," replied Jimmy, with a grin,

"I only wish we had our set finished that we're working on now," said Herb. "Then we ought to get real results."

"It won't take us so very long now," returned Jimmy. "Most of the hard work is done, and all we have to do now is to assemble it, I guess we can get busy at that pretty soon now."

"The sooner the better," answered Herb. "It seems to me that we've been at it an awfully long while."

"Not so long when you consider all the work that there is to a set like that," said Jimmy. "But here we are, and I'm beginning to feel hungry again, although it isn't very long since I had supper. I think I'll hunt around in the kitchen and see if I can't find a few doughnuts. I'm pretty sure that there are some left in the crock."

"I don't see how there can be, if you knew they were there," laughed Herb. "But I hope you do find some. Your mother's doughnuts have a reputation, you know."

"We'll go up to my room first, and then I'll have a look," said Jimmy.

Herb had hardly gotten his coat off before Jimmy returned with several golden brown doughnuts.

"Here we are," he said, triumphantly. "Now to enjoy the radio!"

Herb had brought a pair of ear phones with him, and he and Jimmy connected their phones in series, so that they could both listen at the same time.

They had hardly got settled when they heard the resonant tones of the announcer.

"Mr. Robert Layton will ask a number of conundrums, the answers to come later." So spoke the announcer.

Herb and Jimmy gazed at each other open-mouthed.

"Wh-what did he say?" gasped Jimmy, at length. "Did you hear it the same as I did, Herb?"

"He said Robert Layton, all right!" exclaimed Herb. "What do you suppose——" But here he was interrupted by the well known voice of their friend.

"Give me a pencil!" exclaimed Herb. "I'll guess those before the answers come, or die trying. We can't let Bob get away with this altogether."

"I should say not!" agreed Jimmy, as Herb started scribbling furiously. "I can't believe yet that it's really Bob talking. How do you suppose he ever got on the programme?"

Herb shook his head without stopping his writing, and at last had all the riddles written down.

"Never mind the rest of the programme," he said. "We'll try to solve these things first."

But while they were still struggling to find answers to the knotty riddles, they nearly went over backward in their chairs as another familiar name sounded in their ears. The announcer was giving Joe's name this time, and all Herb and Jimmy could do was to sit and look at each other and mutter inarticulately as Joe recited his selections. When they were over, both boys took off their head phones and gazed solemnly at each other.

"Can you beat it?" asked Herb at length, in a bewildered way.

"Nope," responded Jimmy. "I'm not even going to try. Just think of those two Indians actually getting on a broadcasting programme! I'm knocked so hard that I'll have to eat another doughnut to set me straight again. Finish 'em up, Herb."

And Herb "finished 'em up" while they both ruminated on the incomprehensible vagaries of fate.

"We've got to go over and see 'em do it," declared Jimmy.

"Right you are," returned his chum. "I won't believe it till I see it with my own eyes."

They saw it with their own eyes a week later when the radio boys gave a second performance which was even more successful than the first, since they had got over the nervousness that affected them at the start. The manager renewed his importunities for them to take a regular engagement, assuring them that they had made a decided hit. The best the boys could see their way clear to agree to, however, was to appear one night in each week, and this programme was carried out for the several weeks ensuing, with ever-increasing ability on the part of Bob and Joe and marked satisfaction to the manager of the sending station.

CHAPTER XXV

SOLVING THE MYSTERY

One night after another performance all of the radio boys were waiting in the railroad station when Larry, who had stepped to the news stand to buy a paper, came hurrying back to where they were sitting.

"I've spotted the men who ran me down in the motor boat!" he gasped. "They're talking together over in that corner!"

"Are you sure?" asked Bob, as he looked in the direction indicated.

"Dead sure," declared Larry. "The look I had at them as the motor boat was making for me is engraved on my memory so that I couldn't forget it if I wanted to. Now's the chance to get those fellows jugged. You know the police were looking for them after they ran us down and there's a warrant out for their arrest. The police didn't have their names, so the warrant read for John Doe and

Richard Roe. We've got to act quickly, as they may get up to take a train at any minute."

"Keep your eye on them while I get a station policeman," admonished Bob, as he hurried off.

He found the officer, who listened attentively as he told his story. Then he walked with Bob toward the men who were still engaged in earnest conversation.

As the officer's eyes fell upon them, he gave a start.

"That's Red Pete and Bud McCaffrey, two of the oldest crooks in the business," he said. "They're wanted for more things than that affair of yours. It will be a feather in my cap if I gather them in."

He tightened his grip on the club as he came close to the two men. They looked up at him, and a startled look came into their eyes as they saw his uniform.

"Hello, Pete. Hello, McCaffrey," he greeted them. "I guess you'd better come right along to headquarters. The Chief would like to have a talk with you."

With a snarl the men leaped to their feet and sought to get past the officer. He was too quick for one of them, whom he grabbed by the collar and reduced to submission by two cracks with his club. The other eluded him, however, and promised to make good his escape. But quick as a flash Bob thrust out his foot and tripped him, at the same time falling upon him.

The fall knocked the breath out of the fugitive, and Bob had no trouble in holding him until Joe and the other boys came up, together with another policeman, who had been attracted by the fracas. A patrol wagon was summoned and the prisoners were conveyed to the nearest police station, where they and the bags they had carried were searched in the presence of the boys, who had missed their train in order to be present and give what information they could about the motor boat affair.

The bags were found to contain, among jewelry and other things that were apparently the proceeds of robberies, a number of pawntickets calling for stickpins, watches and other articles which the police lieutenant at the desk announced would be looked up by some of his men. The prisoners were locked up to await a court examination, and the boys, after having given their names and addresses in case they were wanted later on as witnesses, left for home in a state of high excitement over the stirring events of the night.

Bob kept in touch with the case, and a few days later came rushing up to his friends in high glee.

"What do you think, fellows?" he announced. "After the extra performance I gave to-day at the broadcasting station, I dropped in at the police station and had a look at some of the loot the police had gathered up on the strength of the pawntickets. And among them what do you think I saw?"

"The Crown Jewels of England," guessed Herb.

Bob withered him with a look.

"The stickpins and watches of Buck Looker and Carl Lutz!" announced Bob impressively. "Their initials were on the watches."

"Glory be!" cried Larry, who was present. "That clears me in that matter. I know none of you fellows believed Buck's dirty fling, but all the same I've felt uncomfortable ever since."

"Now you'll get a nice letter of apology from Mr. Buck Looker—I don't think," remarked Joe.

The information was conveyed to Buck and Lutz, and they identified and recovered their property. But as Joe had predicted, not a word of apology for their unfounded charges was received from either one of the pair.

Not long afterward the arrested men were convicted and sentenced to long prison terms. It developed that they were old offenders who made a specialty of robbery at summer resorts.

Larry grew steadily better and there was every prospect that his lameness would in time wholly disappear. But he was doing so well at the broadcasting station that he determined to give up any further idea of vaudeville and devote himself to radio, going to a technical school in the meantime to perfect his education. Tim steadily advanced in his chosen vocation, and the boys heard from him frequently. No one rejoiced more than they when they learned that he was at last in the big-time circuit.

During all these events the boys had been busy at developing the receiving set, and at last it was finished to their satisfaction. In the course of their work they gathered a large amount of familiarity with radio which proved of immense value later on, as will be seen in the next volume of this series, entitled: "The Radio Boys at Mountain Pass; Or, The Midnight Call For Assistance."

The special set that represented the advance they had made in radio reception included the regenerative principle. This feature added immensely to the sensitiveness of the set. It consisted of a coil, variously known as the tickler, the intensity coil, and the regeneration coil. It involved three controls, the wave-length tuning, the regenerative coil, and the filament rheostat. The result of the combination was not only that the radio frequency waves could be carried over into the plate circuit, but that they could be amplified there by the energy derived from the local battery in the plate circuit without change of frequency or wave form, and that they could be fed into the grid circuit, where they increased the potential variations on the grid so that the operation constantly repeated itself.

This "feed-back" regeneration enormously increased the loudness of the receiving signals, and its value to the boys was demonstrated one night when the air was unusually free of static and they clearly heard the signals from Nauen, Germany, and the Eiffel Tower, Paris. They looked at each other incredulously at first, and then as they heard the signals again too certainly to admit of doubt, they jumped to their feet, clapped each other on the shoulder, and fairly went wild with delight.

"The first boys in this old town to pick up a message from Europe!" cried Joe. "What next?"

"Asia perhaps," suggested Jimmy.

"Then Australia," ventured Herb.

"Or Mars," predicted Bob. "Who knows?" he added, as he saw the smile of doubt on his comrades' faces. "Marconi thought he might, and he's no dreamer. What is impossible to radio?"

THE END

Made in the USA
Monee, IL
15 August 2021

75749411R00056